Chapter One

"I told you. I'm not doing it."

Sara Anderson stared at the ex-soldier standing on the other side of the half-demolished pasture fence. Matt McCabe had come back from his tour in the Middle East eighteen months ago and, despite the efforts of family and friends to draw him out, had seemed to go deeper into his self-imposed solitude every day.

This kind of moody isolation wasn't good, even for a newly minted Laramie County rancher.

Hadn't she learned that the hard way?

Heaven knew she wasn't going to willingly allow another similar tragedy to happen again. And especially not to someone she'd once been close to, growing up. Not if she could possibly help it, anyway. And she was determined that she could.

Shivering a little in the cool March air, Sara stepped around the heaps of old metal posts and rusting barbed wire strewn across the empty pasture. She plastered an engaging smile on her face while taking in his handsome profile and tall, muscular physique. With his square jaw and gorgeously chiseled features, Matt had always been mesmerizing. Even when, like now, he did not put much effort into his appearance. His clothes were old, clean and rumpled. Boots scuffed and coated with mud.

The dark brown hair peeking out from under the brim of his black Resistol was a little on the long side, curling across his brow and over his ears, down the nape of his neck. And though he had clearly showered that morning, he hadn't shaved in days. All of which, combined, gave him a hopelessly rugged, masculine look.

The kind that set her heart racing.

And shouldn't have.

Given the fact she had definitely not come here to flirt or see where the age-old attraction between them would lead. An attraction they hadn't ever dared to explore, even in their reckless high school days.

Sara drew a breath. Tried again. Picking up the conversation where they'd left off.

"And I told you—" with effort, she held his stormy gray-blue eyes "—I'm not giving up." She was determined to enlist his help…and save him along the way.

With a scoff, Matt swaggered away from her, his strides long and lazy. He bent to pick up the pieces of a wood fence post scattered across the field, then tossed them into the bed of his battered Silver Creek Ranch pickup truck. "Well, you should retreat," he advised over one broad, chambray-clad shoulder. His dark brow lifted in a warning that set her pulse racing all the more. "'Cause I'm not changing my mind."

Like heck he wasn't!

His Baby Bargain

Cathy Gillen Thacker

H HARLEQUIN® SPECIAL EDITION

Recycling programs
for this product may
not exist in your area.

ISBN-13: 978-1-335-57381-0

His Baby Bargain

Copyright © 2019 by Cathy Gillen Thacker

HARLEQUIN®
www.Harlequin.com

Printed in U.S.A.

Cathy Gillen Thacker is married and a mother of three. She and her husband spent eighteen years in Texas and now reside in North Carolina. Her mysteries, romantic comedies and heartwarming family stories have made numerous appearances on bestseller lists, but her best reward, she says, is knowing one of her books made someone's day a little brighter. A popular Harlequin author for many years, she loves telling passionate stories with happy endings and thinks nothing beats a good romance and a hot cup of tea! You can visit Cathy's website, cathygillenthacker.com, for more information on her upcoming and previously published books, recipes and a list of her favorite things.

Books by Cathy Gillen Thacker

Harlequin Special Edition

Texas Legends: The McCabes

The Texas Cowboy's Quadruplets

Harlequin Western Romance

Texas Legends: The McCabes

The Texas Cowboy's Triplets
The Texas Cowboy's Baby Rescue

Texas Legacies: The Lockharts

A Texas Soldier's Family
A Texas Cowboy's Christmas
The Texas Valentine Twins

Visit the Author Profile page
at Harlequin.com for more titles.

To Dylan, my favorite chocolate Labrador retriever
and the newest member of the Thacker clan.
Her puppy antics and gentle, intelligent nature
were the inspiration for Champ,
the black Lab puppy in this book.

Sara put on her most persuasive smile and stalked through the knee-high grass and the Texas wildflowers getting ready to bloom. "Never say never," she warned cheerfully. Especially when she had set her mind to something this important.

Matt pushed back the brim of his hat with his index finger. Brazenly looked her up and down in a way that heated her flesh, head to toe. "And why is that?" he challenged softly.

Sara focused on the nonprofit organization and the ex-soldiers she was helping. Her actions every bit as deliberate as his, she moved closer still. "Because if you ever deign to meet him, you just might fall in love with Champ, the remaining black Lab puppy from the latest West Texas Warriors Association's litter." She certainly had. Not that she was signing up to train a service dog. Not when she would soon be going back to work as a large-animal veterinarian and had a six-month-old son to raise.

Matt folded his arms across his muscular chest and let out a sigh that reverberated through his entire six-foot-three-inch frame. "Good thing I'm not planning on visiting the puppy, then."

Time to play the guilt card, and appeal to the legendary McCabe chivalry. "You're seriously opposed to helping out other returning military veterans in need of a therapy dog?"

Irritation darkened his eyes and he pressed his sensual lips into a thin, hard line. "Of course not." He gestured offhandedly. "Just tell me where to send the check and…"

She held up a staying palm. "We've got money, Matt." At least for the needs of the current litters. "What we *need* are more hands-on trainers to help socialize the puppies."

His expression grew even more impatient. "Well, that's not me," he countered curtly. "Haven't you heard? I'm not exactly a dog person these days."

Actually, she had learned he'd become mysteriously averse to pets. Which was strange. When they'd grown up together, there hadn't been an animal who didn't automatically gravitate to the personable cowboy with the exquisitely gentle touch.

Deciding to call him out on this—and anything else that needed to be challenged—she scoffed, "Oh yeah. Since when?" What had happened to him in the time he'd been away from Laramie County? That had made him decide to clear a two thousand acre ranch, all on his own?

Their eyes met, held. For a moment, the years of near estrangement faded and she thought he might answer, but the opportunity passed, with nary a word.

Matt squinted right back at her. Shrugged. "I've got a question, too, darlin'." Deliberately, he stepped into her personal space. "When did *you* get so darned pesky?"

The endearment, coupled with the insult, worked just as Matt hoped.

Sara's slender shoulders stiffened and she drew herself up to her full five feet, nine inches. She glared at him resentfully. "I've always been extremely helpful and forthright!"

He grunted and reached for the metal cutters. Walking along the fence, he snipped through the lengths of rusting barbed wire. Irritated to find she was still fast on his heels.

"Is that what they're calling your do-gooding these

days?" He slanted a glance at her, and noted the way the breeze was plastering the soft knit of her sweater against her delectable breasts. Ignoring the hardening of his body, he turned his gaze back to her face. "And here I was thinking you were just bossy and interfering."

She dug her boots into the hard ground beneath them and propped both her hands on her denim-clad hips. "I go where I'm needed, Matt."

The fact she, like so many others close to him, apparently saw him as a charity case rankled. Gathering up the wire, he walked back to toss it into the bed of his pickup truck alongside the stack of weathered metal posts. "I don't remember calling for a large-animal vet."

She continued shadowing him, getting close enough he could inhale the lilac of her perfume. "Then I guess it's your lucky day," she announced. "Me, showing up here—"

"Uninvited," he turned to point out.

She held her ground. "—and all."

This ornery woman had no idea who she was playing with. "Uh-huh." Matt moved closer, drinking in her fair skin and sun-blushed cheeks. Damn, she was pretty, standing there in the spring sunlight. Her cloud of golden-blond hair drifting across her shoulders and framing the delicate features of her face.

In an effort to further repel her, he let his gaze move lower, to the lithe build of her body. From her dainty feet and long sexy legs, to her slender waist and the lush fullness of her breasts, she was all woman.

Still enjoying the view immensely, he returned his focus to the elegance of her lips, cheeks and nose. The jade depths of her eyes. "Sure you're in the right place? Talking to the right ex-soldier?"

"Definitely." She trod even closer and tilted her chin up to his. "And believe it or not, I'm strong enough to handle you, cowboy."

"Sure about that?" Matt asked gruffly, wishing he hadn't noticed how feminine and perfect she was. All over.

"Yes," she repeated.

Funny. She hadn't seemed strong when she'd lost her husband a little over a year before. She'd seemed vulnerable. Achingly so.

To the point, every time he'd run into her, he'd been tempted to take her in his arms and hold her close. Not as the platonic friends they'd once been in their high school days. But as an ex-soldier comforting another ex-soldier's wife.

There were several problems with that. First, he'd already gone down that route before—and learned the hard way that any relationship based on rebound emotions was a huge mistake.

And second, she was so damn pretty and accomplished these days, he knew he'd never be able to leave it at that. Holding Sara close would make him want things he couldn't have and had no business wanting.

Because, thanks to the mistakes he'd made and the guilt he still harbored, having a wife or a family of his own was no longer in the cards for him.

Clearly misunderstanding the reason behind his long pause, Sara pleated her brow. She looked at him more closely, then queried cautiously, "Really, Matt? You seriously *doubt* my inner strength?"

"No," he conceded honestly. "You're as feisty as they come."

"Feisty," she said, repeating the term distastefully. "Really."

He grinned, thrilled to be getting under her skin.

It was that friction that would help keep them apart.

Watching the color come into her high, sculpted cheeks, he removed his hat and let it fall idly against his thigh. "Don't like the term?"

Her pretty green eyes narrowing, she watched him run his fingers through his hair. "It's condescending!"

He settled his Resistol squarely back on his head. "Yeah?" he retorted sardonically. "In what way?" Because she was feisty and then some. Always had been.

Oblivious to how much he liked her spirit, Sara let out a lengthy sigh. "In the sense that *feisty* is an adjective usually attached to a female or small animal one would *not* expect to defend itself."

He rolled his eyes at her deliberately haughty tone. "Spoken like a veterinarian," he said. Then seeing a way to needle her further, added, "A *woman* veterinarian."

Now she was spitting mad. She planted her hands on her hips again. "You just keep digging yourself in deeper, don't you, cowboy?"

He shrugged in a way designed to rankle her even more. "Hey. If it annoys you, maybe you should leave." He went back to pull up some more aging fence posts.

"Not until you at least agree to come to my ranch and see the puppy."

He turned so suddenly she nearly slammed into him. He inhaled another whiff of her lilac perfume. "Why me?" he asked as his gaze drifted over her fitted suede jacket and dark, figure-hugging jeans. "Instead of someone else a hell of a lot more amenable?"

Sara sighed and folded her arms beneath her breasts, her action plumping them up all the more. "Because we need more veterans actively involved in helping other returning military personnel," she stated softly, her breasts rising and falling with each agitated breath.

He rocked back on the heels of his worn leather work boots. "Isn't that the mission of the West Texas Warriors Association?" Of which, he knew, there were hundreds of members.

Her expression turned even more serious. "We need everyone, Matt."

He rejected her attempt to make him feel guilty for not wanting to dive back into the world of his nightmares. "I don't think so."

She glowered at him. "Why not?"

"I like my solitude."

She made a face and then, to his mounting frustration, tried again. "Listen to me, Matt," she beseeched, hands outstretched. Her gentle eyes filled with compassion. "I know how hard it was for Anthony to really reconnect after he came back to civilian life…"

So, the rumors about her late husband's unhappiness…and maybe hers, too…were true.

He scowled, not sure why the comparison bothered him so much. "I'm not your late husband, Sara."

She acknowledged that with a nod, then pushed on despite his gruff, unwelcoming tone. "Working with dogs can help alleviate PTSD-related depression and anxiety."

Now what is she trying to infer? "Do tell," he prodded.

She tilted her head to one side and offered a tantalizing smile. "Who knows?" Another shrug. "It might help right your temperamental attitude, too."

Not sure whether he wanted to haul her close and kiss her, or demand she leave *now*, he sent her a censuring look. "Thanks, but I've got my bad moods covered, Sara."

She huffed, her eyes narrowing all the more. "Spending all your time alone?"

"Making the Silver Creek Ranch a cash-generating enterprise," he corrected.

Sara seemed unimpressed. "By tearing down tons of trees and ripping down sections of old fence?"

He went back to snipping barbed wire. "First of all, the fence is so old it's a hazard. Second, Texas barbecue restaurants need either oak or mesquite. And I've got plenty of both."

Sara tapped one boot-clad foot impatiently. "And then what? When you clear-cut all this land?"

She sounded like his folks. Constantly complaining that whatever he was doing wasn't enough.

He yanked out a rusting metal post and added it to the pile on the ground. "I'm going to plow the weeds and sow some grass. Put up new pasture fence and lease out the land to my brother Cullen so he can run some of his cattle here."

Giving him room to work, she took a moment to consider that. Probably finally realizing he did indeed have a business plan.

"Not planning to buy any of your own?" she asked eventually.

He shook his head. The last thing he wanted was to be responsible for another living thing—person or animal. "Did enough cattle herding growing up."

That, she did seem to understand. It didn't mean she let up. Her gorgeous honey-blond hair blowing in the spring breeze, she followed him down the fence line. "You know, you could do all this a lot faster if you hired some help. Or even enlisted some of your family members and friends."

Her unsolicited advice irked him. He turned and studied the guileless look in her eyes. "Don't want me to be alone, huh, darlin'?"

She pursed her lips in a worried frown. "I don't think it's healthy and neither does your family, Matt."

So now they were finally getting down to it, he thought wearily.

She stepped closer, once again invading his space.

Her soft, feminine voice took on a persuasive lilt. "Your mom came to see me. She thought maybe I could talk you into rejoining the community again."

Matt shook his head at Sara's naïveté. His mom hoped for a lot more than occasionally getting him off the Silver Creek spread. "She only did that because…"

Sara beamed, turning on the full wattage of her neighborly charm. "What?"

He edged closer. "She knows I'm attracted to you."

She laughed in disbelief, the ambivalent sound filling the air between them. Her lower lip took on a kissable pout. "You're just saying that to get me to leave."

He surveyed her indignant expression. Leaned in closer. "Is it working?"

The look in her eyes grew turbulent. "No."

He dropped his head. "Then how about this?" he taunted softly, taking her in his arms.

Rather than step away, she put her hand on the center of his chest, and gave him a small, purposeful shove.

That sent him exactly nowhere.

"No." She glared at him heatedly. "But nice try, cowboy."

He reluctantly let her go and stepped back, his own temper flaring. "Then maybe you should rethink this plan you and my mom cooked up. Because I'm not the guy who's going to treat you with kid gloves, darlin'."

And he was pretty sure, at the end of the day, that was what Sara wanted.

Her eyes narrowed. "I don't want you to treat me with kid gloves."

He came back to her, took her in his arms again and lowered his lips, just above hers.

Damn, if she didn't make him feel ornery.

He smiled as she caught her breath. "Sure about that?" He rubbed the pad of his thumb across her lower lip.

Her brows furrowed as she began to see where this standoff between them was likely headed. "Yes," she said, stubborn as ever, trembling even as she held her ground.

Loving the delicate feel of her body so close to his, he asked, "Really sure?"

"Completely sure," she taunted right back. "In fact, cowboy," she went on to dare in spunky delight, "you could *kiss* me and—"

The gauntlet had been thrown down between them.

Matt never gave her a chance to blurt out the rest.

His mouth touched hers, laying claim to every sweet soft inch. Only, the indignant slap he expected—the one that would have heralded his immediate gentlemanly release of her, and her quick, fiery exit—never came.

Sara told herself to resist the sensual feel of his lips moving over hers. But her body refused to listen to the wary dictates of her heart. She had been numb inside for so long. Responsive only to the needs of her adorable infant son.

Now, suddenly, she was alive in a way she had never expected to be again. The yearning to be touched, held, appreciated for the woman she was came roaring back.

Made her tingle all over. Opening her lips to his, she pressed closer to the unyielding hardness of his chest, and, lower still, felt his undeniable heat and building desire. With a low moan of surrender, she went up on tiptoe, wreathed her arms about his neck and tilted her head to give him deeper access. He uttered a low moan of approval. His tongue twined with hers. He brought her nearer still, delivering a kiss that scored her soul. Left her limp with longing and trembling with acquiescence. Her middle fluttering, she melted against him. And then all was lost, as she experienced the masculine force that was Matt. For the first time in her life, she was with a man who didn't hesitate to give her the complete physicality she craved and had always longed to explore. Excitement roaring through her, she reveled in the thrill of his commanding embrace. The hard, insistent pressure of his kiss, and the tantalizing sweep of his tongue; for the very first time in her life, she experienced the temptation to surrender herself completely. Forget her worries about the future. Live only in the moment she was in.

Had her life not already been so complicated—full of the grief and guilt she still felt for not doing as much as she could have, or should have, when she'd still had the chance—and had she not intuited that Matt's own private world was much the same as hers and her husband's had once been, who knew what might have happened had their make-out session continued on this brisk and sunny spring day?

But they did both harbor secrets and heartache.

And combining the two would only risk further hurt. For her, for him, for her baby boy.

So she did what she should have done all along, and

finally put her hand on the center of his chest and tore her lips from his.

Just that quickly, Matt let her go.

They stared at each other, breathing hard. To her surprise, he looked every bit as shaken as she felt.

Compelled to save them both and downplay this, however, she took another step back. Gave a hapless shrug, looked into his eyes and said, "Just so you know, cowboy, you're not the first man who's made a move on me since Anthony died."

He was the first one who'd made her feel something, though. Too much, actually. Way too much.

Emotion warred with the skepticism in his eyes. "Trying to make me feel competitive?"

No! Heck, no! Sara thought, chagrined. "I'm just saying," she returned as calmly as possible, "I wasn't interested then. And I'm not interested now."

The corners of his lips turned up as his gaze raked her luxuriantly, head to toe. "Your kisses just said otherwise, darlin'."

Once again, she shook her head. Embarrassed. Humiliated. And worst of all, still wildy turned on. Swallowing around the ache in her throat, she held his eyes deliberately and corrected him. "My kisses said I'm human, Matt." *Human and oh so lonely, deep down. So ready to get out of my own misery and help someone else in need. Like you, Matt. And how crazy is that?*

She waited a moment to let her words sink in. Then said, "As are we all."

It didn't mean she had to be a fool for a second time.

And especially not with the far too irresistible Matt McCabe.

Chapter Two

"Is this a good time?" Matt asked, from the porch of Sara's Blue Vista Ranch house the following Saturday afternoon.

For you, Matt McCabe, Sara thought, still reeling from the hot, audacious kisses he had delivered the last time they'd seen each other, *there will never be a good time. Not ever again.*

But not about to let him know how much he had affected her, or how often and passionately she'd thought of him over the last week, she merely looked him up and down.

The reality was, he was the last person she had expected to see standing on her doorstep, given how acrimoniously they had last parted.

But here he was, as mouthwateringly handsome as ever. Looking mighty fine in a blue button-down shirt that made the most of his brawny shoulders and rock-solid abs. New jeans that did equally appetizing things to his long, muscular legs and hips, and shiny brown boots. He'd shaved and showered, too, although his thick, wavy dark brown hair was just as unruly as she'd come to expect. His dark gray-blue eyes just as wryly challenging.

"Depends on why you're here," she replied tartly, wishing she were clad in something other than a peach tunic and white yoga pants stained with drool and baby formula. She looked down her nose at him, pausing to make sure he knew just how unwelcome he was. "If it's to pick up where we left off last week…"

His sensual lips lifted into a tantalizing smile. Excitement lit his eyes. "Kissing you?"

She flushed at the memory of his delicious body pressed against hers, his lips stirring up needs best forgotten. She was a widow, after all. Determined to never make the mistake of turning her heart over to a man again.

Never mind the strong, silent, stubborn type.

"Arguing."

He chuckled and ran a hand across his jaw. A wicked grin deepened the crinkles around his eyes. "Is that what we were doing?" he drawled, tilting his head.

So she wasn't the only one who'd been remembering! Huffing in aggravation, Sara folded her arms tightly in front of her. "Let's just say our discussion made me realize you and I will *never* be on the same page, McCabe." And she refused to chase after lost causes, so…

An infant wail went up from somewhere behind her. Sara tensed in distress and lifted a staying hand.

Saved by the baby.

"Hang on a minute." She rushed off to gather up her son and returned with the red-faced infant in her arms, ready to direct Matt on his way. Instead, she found him looking down at her little boy with surprising interest.

"This Charley?" Matt asked tenderly, taking in her son's sturdy little body, cherubic features and shock of fine blond hair. The long-lashed eyes that had started out blue and were now more dark green.

Surprised, Sara asked, "You know his name?"

Matt shrugged as he and Charley locked gazes and the infant momentarily stopped crying, then ever so slowly began to smile. "I know a lot of things," he murmured.

Charley reached for Matt, and when Matt offered his hand, the baby latched on tight to the tall cowboy's pinky.

In the same soothing tone that would have done a baby wrangler proud, Matt continued, "Including the fact you've told everyone to give up on ever getting me involved in the West Texas Warrior Association's therapy-puppy raising program."

Sara had indeed put out the word.

Figuring there was no reason to stand in the doorway while they talked, she ushered him in. He shut the door dutifully behind them. "And that bothers you because…?"

Sara perched on the edge of the living room sofa, a little embarrassed by the mess around them. She settled Charley on her lap, while Matt—who still had his hand linked in Charley's little fist—settled next to them.

Exhaling, the handsome cowboy looked deep into her eyes. "Since you talked to my mom, every member of my family has come out to the Silver Creek to see me."

Glad to see the indomitable Matt off-kilter for once, Sara grinned. "What's the matter, cowboy?" she teased, knowing there wasn't a finer group than Rachel and Frank McCabe and their offspring. "Don't like family?"

Appearing more besotted than ever of the tall rugged man with the deep, soothing voice, Charley reached up to hold on to Matt with both of his little hands.

Matt grinned down at her son, looking happier than Sara could recall in a long, long time.

Apparently realizing he hadn't answered her question, Matt let out a long exhalation of breath, then turned his attention back to her once again. "I love 'em," he said, before adding, "when they're minding their own business."

Sara regarded him pensively. She understood that. She had two college-professor parents and five older brothers who'd been in her business for years. Fortunately, all of them were now scattered across the country, busy living their own lives. And though she could have relocated next to any of them after Anthony died, she had chosen to stay on the small ranch where they had hoped to bring up Charley.

Part of that had been because she still considered the rural Texas county where she had grown up home, and hadn't wanted the stress of finding another job at another veterinary practice and another place to live.

The rest had to do with her not wanting to clue any of them in on the private misery she'd been unable to share with anyone. Least of all those who might have judged her for not being the kind of wife she should have been.

But her own heartache had nothing to do with Matt's problems now. She settled Charley a little more comfortably on her lap and drew a breath. "I get you have a problem, McCabe, but I don't see where I come in."

Charley finally let go of Matt's finger.

Matt got up and paced over to the fireplace, stood with his back to it, admitting gruffly, "The problem is they're not going to give up on what they want for me."

Sara saw where that would be a problem for a man

who professed to only want to be left alone. She bit her lip, acutely aware that things were getting way too intimate between them again, way too fast. "What? Can't kiss them to make them go away?" she quipped.

He let out a belly laugh.

At the low masculine sound, so foreign in Sara's small cottage-style bungalow, Charley's brows knit together. He began to cry again, so heartrendingly this time it was all Sara could do to swallow the lump in her throat.

First she had failed as a wife. And now, this…

Matt frowned in alarm.

Sara's lack of sleep made her own eyes well, too. She stood and began to walk the floor with Charley, jostling him a little as she moved in the hopes that the slight, swaying motion would soothe him. It did not.

"What's wrong with him?" Matt asked.

That was the bitter irony. "I don't know." And as his mother, she certainly should have. She rocked him back and forth.

Matt strode closer, his handsome features etched with tenderness. He lifted his hand to Charley. This time, the baby howled all the louder and batted Matt's palm away.

"Then why is he so fussy?" Matt had to speak up to be heard over the wailing.

Sara arched a brow, irritated to have him constantly finding ways to make her feel off balance, not to mention seeming more inept than she already was. "If I knew that, do you really think he'd still be crying?" she demanded.

Ignoring her pique, Matt gently touched her son's cheek, as if checking for fever. Again, Charley batted his hand away.

Taking the cue, Matt backed off. "Is he sick?"

Glad to have someone to share her concern with,

Sara shifted Charley to her other shoulder. She continued gently soothing him, as best she could. Looking over his blond head at Matt, she admitted, "I thought he might be since he's so cranky and doesn't want to eat, but he doesn't have any fever. He's not pulling at his ears the way he did when he had an ear infection, either."

"Is his throat red?" Matt asked, while Charley warmed to the audience and wailed even louder.

Was this what it would be like to have someone big and strong and male to share the parenting duties with? Telling herself she was really losing it, Sara pushed the ridiculous notion away. "I can't answer that, either. I haven't been able to get a good look." And in fact, she had been considering going into the emergency pediatric clinic in town, if this went on much longer.

Matt pointed out, "His mouth is open now."

Figuring as long as she had help she might as well use it, she retrieved the flashlight she kept on the kitchen counter. Then turned back to Matt. "You want to hold him?"

For the first time, Matt hesitated.

"Listen, cowboy, either be part of the solution or leave. Because I don't need any more problems today."

From the pen in the corner of the living room, Champ, the nine-week-old black Labrador puppy Sara had been trying to get Matt to help socialize, lifted his head and began to jump up against the three-foot wooden sides of the whelping pen, in rhythm to Charley's wails.

Matt turned in the direction of the noise. He locked eyes on the puppy.

And in that instant, Sara knew.

Matt wasn't a dog person.

Not in the slightest.

Not anymore.

* * *

Matt swore silently to himself as he clamped down on the memories he worked so hard to quash.

When he'd set out for Sara's ranch, he'd figured he would see her baby. He'd even been sort of looking forward to it. Why, he couldn't exactly say.

He hadn't figured she'd have one of the pups from the litter there. But she did and as the puppy continued whimpering with excitement and trying to climb over the sides, it was all he could do not to break out into an ice-cold sweat.

Over a harmless little black Lab pup, of all things.

"Matt?" Sara's hand was on his arm. Her tone as gentle as it was inquiring.

"Sorry," he rasped, turning his back to the rambunctious retriever. "I'll hold Charley while you try and get a look at your son's throat."

Ignoring the stuff of his nightmares, Matt held out his arms. Sara shifted her son over. Oblivious to Matt's private grief come to life, Charley wailed even louder.

Whatever questions she had—and she seemed to have plenty—could wait.

On task once again, Sara cupped her son's chin in her hand and shined the flashlight in that direction. While the puppy gave up trying to escape, opting instead to pick up a squeaky toy and then roll happily around with it in the pen, Charley twisted his head to the side, buried his head in Matt's chest and firmly clamped his lips shut.

Sara seemed even more nonplussed.

"Why don't you hold him? I'll look," Matt said.

Nodding in frustration, Sara set the flashlight down and took Charley back in her arms. The moment she had him, he glared at her, as if he blamed *her* for whatever was bothering him, and began to howl again, even more vociferously.

Matt hunched so he was at eye level with Charley—and trained the light low, so it only hit the lower half of her son's face. He surveyed the back of his throat. "Looks fine," Matt said in surprise. The way Charley was carrying on, he'd expected to find it beet red. "A healthy normal pink."

"No spots? Even on the roof of his mouth? Red or white?"

Matt looked again, as Charley began to cry in earnest once again. "Not a one."

"Oh, Charley, honey, what's wrong?" Sara said, swaying her little boy back and forth.

Noting the puppy was now drinking water, and vastly relieved his own unexpected memories were now subsiding, Matt whipped out his phone. "How old is Charley?"

Sara shifted her son onto her shoulder and walked over to the puppy pen. She reached down to give Champ another toy to occupy him. Turning back to face Matt, said, "He turned six months old ten days ago."

Figuring the sooner he was able to get out of there, the better, he punched in a number.

Sara came closer, a still-whimpering Charley cradled in her arms. As she attempted to see what he was doing, her shoulder bumped up against the center of his chest. "Who are you calling?"

"Cullen's wife, Bridgett."

His brother's wife was a neonatal nurse at Laramie Community Hospital, and a mother to a one-year-old boy, with another child on the way. Luckily, she answered right away. "Hey," he said. "I'm at Sara Anderson's ranch, and we've got a little problem…"

While Matt described what was going on, Sara carried Charley into the kitchen and got a bottle of apple juice out of the fridge. She offered it to the baby. Still sniffling, he took it in his chubby little hands, put it in his mouth and started to sip, then let out another wail and pushed it away.

Matt came back. He hated to pry, but Bridgett needed to know if she was to help. "Are you still nursing?"

As he spoke, his eyes slid to her breasts. Although it was a natural reaction on his part, Sara flushed self-consciously.

"I switched him to formula when I had the flu last month."

Averting his glance, Matt relayed that, too.

By the time he'd turned back to her, Sara had composed herself once again. "Bridgett said to check his gums to see if they are red or swollen or if there is any sign of a tooth pushing through. She said sometimes they can teethe for a few days or weeks before the tooth actually shows."

Sara ventured a look, but Charley pressed his lips shut again. With maternal resolve, she eased the tip of her index fingertip along the seam of his lips, trying to gently persuade him to open up. Eventually he did. Just enough so she could get her finger between his gums.

With a scowl, Charley clamped down tight.

"Ouch!" Sara winced in surprise.

"Feel a tooth?"

"No." She shifted Charley a little higher in her arms, so they were face-to-face. Now that he'd bitten her, he was beginning to look a little more content. Satisfied he'd gotten his point across, maybe? Matt wondered.

"But," she mused as she pulled his lower lip down,

"his gum does look a tiny bit swollen here on the bottom. Right here in the middle."

Matt relayed the information then said, "Bridgett wants to talk to you." He set his cell phone aside while he eased Charley from her arms. "I can't believe I didn't even think of that," Sara told his sister-in-law.

He walked the little boy back and forth, while the two women talked. Eventually, Sara hung up. She walked into the kitchen and took a children's medical kit from the cupboard. "Bridgett said their son Robby's first tooth caught them by surprise, too."

"I remember."

"She said to try numbing medicine."

"Hear that, little guy? Your mommy is going to fix you right up."

Charley lounged against his broad chest. Tears still gleaming damply on his cheeks, he gazed up at Matt adoringly. Sara turned back to Matt as she worked the protective seal off the numbing cream. "You're good with little ones," she remarked.

He shrugged, aware that was a talent he came by naturally. "You know the McCabes. Lots of little ones around. Seems like someone is always putting a baby in my arms."

Sara regarded him skeptically. "You could say no," she pointed out wryly.

Lately, he usually did. Trying not to wonder why he hadn't in this particular case, Matt shrugged again and turned his attention to sparring with his old friend. "Actually, darlin'," he drawled, "I believe I do refuse things every now and again." He lifted his brow, reminding. "Like your repeated requests to recruit me for the therapy-puppy training program?"

She came close enough to rub a little medicine on Charley's gum. Her son wrinkled his nose, too surprised to protest. As the moment drew out, Charley's jaw relaxed and his little shoulders slumped in relief.

So his mouth had been hurting, Matt thought. Poor little fella.

Without warning, Charley held out his arms to his mommy. Reluctantly, Matt transferred the little boy, surprised to find how bereft he felt when he was no longer holding him.

Wordlessly, he watched Sara cuddle her baby boy. They were the picture of bliss. Enough to make him want, just for one ill-advised second, a wife and child of his own to love and care for...

Sara tossed him a wry glance. "Speaking of the WTWA therapy-puppy raising program...if you gave yourself half a chance, I bet you would be really good with our puppies, too."

Just like that, his genial mood faded. "No," he said firmly. "I won't."

Once again, Matt noted, he had disappointed Sara. Deeply.

Seeing the puppy circling in the pen, Sara handed Charley back to Matt and rushed to pick up the sleek little black Lab. She carried him outside to the grass next to her ranch house.

"Then why are you here, if not to volunteer to train a puppy as I asked?"

Matt positioned Charley so he could see outward, and then held him against his chest, one of his forearms acting as the seat for the baby's diaper-clad bottom, the other serving as a safety harness across his tiny chest.

He shrugged. "I wanted to give money. You said you needed more volunteers, especially military. I want to *fund* an effort to recruit and train more puppy handlers."

He expected her to immediately jump at his offer. She didn't.

"For someone who has been adamantly opposed to becoming involved in any way with the therapy and service dog program, this is quite the turnaround," Sara stated, looking him up and down with the same savvy she'd exhibited in years past. "What's the catch?"

Of course she would figure out he had an ulterior motive. Matt proposed, "You let my family know that I've become 'involved' so they'll stop haranguing me."

Sara sent a glance heavenward. "I'm not sure they'll consider writing a check *involved*, cowboy." She mimicked his deadpan tone. "But you do have a good idea. Especially if we were to combine the recruiting efforts with the first annual WTWA service-dog reunion picnic we're hosting in a few weeks."

Aware that sounded like more than he could handle, without triggering a whole new slew of nightmares, Matt lifted his hand. "Listen, I'll help out with anything that needs to be done organizationally…"

Her eyes glittering with disappointed, Sara seemed to guess where this was going. "But you still don't want to help in the hands-on socialization of Champ."

"No." Aware the pup had finished peeing and was hopping around his feet, begging to be picked up, Matt steadfastly ignored him. "Not my thing."

Sara picked up a ball and threw it, then watched Champ bound off to retrieve it. "What's happened to you? I don't remember you having an aversion to animals growing up."

The truth was he hadn't.

"Did you get bit or attacked by a dog or something?"

Once again she knew him too well. Despite the time that had elapsed since they'd been friends.

"No."

She peered at him in concern. "Lose one you cared about so deeply that you can't bear to be around another?"

Comforted by the feel of Charley snuggled up against him, Matt pushed away the unwanted emotions welling up inside of him. "I told you. I don't have the patience to train a puppy."

"Really?" she echoed skeptically. "Because you seem to have a lot of patience with my son." Her gaze drifted over him and Charley before she tossed the ball again.

He turned his attention to the close fit of her white yoga pants over her spectacular legs, and felt his body harden. "It's different."

She continued to study him as Champ raced off.

His gaze drifted up to her peach knit tunic top. The fit was looser, but it still did a nice job of showing off her luscious breasts and trim midriff. He liked the half-moon necklace and matching earrings she wore, too.

In fact, liked everything about her. Maybe too much.

"Something's going on with you," she persisted.

He cut her off brusquely. Not about to go down that path. "I don't have PTSD, if that's what you're inferring."

She regarded him with steely intent. "Sure about that? I heard your last tour was pure hell. That's why you quit the army when your commitment was up."

He shrugged. "I came back. I'm alive."

Another telling lift of her delicate brow.

"Maybe the question, then, is," she countered softly, "who didn't?"

Again, right on point.

Silence fell.

Wondering if it would always be like this between them—her challenging, him resisting—he said nothing more.

The puppy came over, panting. Sara gathered him in her arms. "Time to eat, buddy."

Matt followed her inside. Figuring it was his turn to question her on her choices, he said, "I'm surprised you took on a puppy when you already have your hands full with Charley."

She filled a food bowl and set it back inside the whelping pen, next to the water bowl and the puppy. "I didn't plan to, but Alyssa Barnes, the soldier who was going to raise Champ and help with his training, had a setback." She straightened and went to the sink to wash her hands, then came back to him and took Charley in her arms.

"She's going to be in the hospital another week, and then a rehab facility here in Laramie for about twenty-one days after that," she explained. "But she still wants to do it, and I'm not about to take that away from her, when this is all she's been looking forward to. And since you wouldn't even consider helping me, cowboy, even on a short-term basis, I volunteered myself."

Guilt flooded Matt. Along with the surprising need to have her understand where he was coming from. He trod closer, appreciating the sight of Charley nestled contentedly against her breasts. Noting how sweet they looked, he spread his hands wide. "Look, it's not that I'm selfish or heartless." He drew a deep breath and confessed what he had yet to admit to anyone else. "I just don't want to be around dogs, okay?" Even one as technically cute and lively as little Champ.

She settled Charley in his high chair, persistent as ever. "And again I have to ask… Why is that, Matt? What's changed?"

Annoyed, he watched her snap a bib around Charley's neck. Wishing he didn't want to haul her against him and kiss her again. Never more so than when they sparred.

Working to keep his emotional distance, he let his glance sift over her in a way he knew annoyed her, then challenged, "Why do you care?"

Especially after she'd already told everyone she was giving up on him. And walking away…

A fact that had somehow irked him.

"I don't know." She plucked a banana from the bunch. Looked over at him and sighed. "Maybe it's because I feel disrespected by you."

Disrespected! "In what sense?" He'd come here to extend the olive branch. Not drive her away with bad behavior the way he had a week ago. And yet here they were, bringing out the worst in each other…again…

Setting the peeled banana on a plate, she frowned and said, "In the sense that people tend to not tell me sad or upsetting stories since Anthony died." She raked a hand through her hair, pushing it off her face. "It's as if they're afraid that I'm so fragile, if they say or do the wrong thing, they'll push me over the edge."

He lounged against the counter, opposite Charley. He empathized with her. "I'm familiar with the walking-on-eggshells part."

She wheeled her son's high chair closer to the breakfast table, sat down and began to mash the fruit with a fork. "Then you can also understand my frustration at having apparently been tasked with getting your help and yet simultaneously been cut out of the loop. Because there is clearly something more going on here than what I'd been told."

He could see she felt blindsided, when all she'd been trying to do was help. The wounded vet, Alyssa Barnes. Him. Champ. And in that sense, he did owe her. So…he drew up a chair on the other side of Charley, sat down and said, "You want to know what happened?"

She nodded, expression tense.

Matt gulped. "I saw a dog get blown up right in front of me." *And worse…* "His death was my fault."

Chapter Three

Sara stared at Matt, hardly able to comprehend what he had just said. "And your family knows you were a part of such a terrible tragedy?" she asked, aghast. Or more horrifying still, that he felt *personally* responsible?

His expression closed and inscrutable, Matt watched her begin to feed her son. "I'm not really sure what they know."

Sara spooned up a bit of mashed banana from Charley's chin. "But you haven't told them," she ascertained quietly.

As he exhaled, his broad shoulders tensed, then relaxed. "It would freak my mom and dad out to know how close I came to dying. So no, I didn't give them any specifics other than what was reported in the news. That our base was hit by suicide bombers in the middle of the night. And there were no injuries or fatalities among our soldiers."

Thank heaven for that, she thought. Resisting the urge to jump up and hug him fiercely *only* because she thought such a move would be rejected, she asked, "Was it a bomb-sniffing dog who saved you?"

"No," Matt said hoarsely. "Mutt was one of a half dozen strays we picked up over there and took in."

Sara caught the note of raw emotion in his voice. She slanted Matt another empathetic glance, then rose and got two bottles of water from the fridge. "The army lets you do that?"

He tilted his head. "It depends on the commanding officer and the situation." Matt relaxed when Charley turned and grinned at him. He stuck out his hand, and Charley latched on to his palm, banging it up and down on the tray. "Our CO thought having dogs around was good for morale. Reminded us of home. Gave us something other than the war to think about."

Sara could see that. Relieved that he was finally confiding in her, she walked back to join Matt and her son at the breakfast table.

"So he let us keep them and train them, but no one person was allowed to adopt any one dog. The deal was the pets belonged to the unit, and we had to rotate their care," Matt related. "Anyone who was interested could sign up, and on the day and night you were assigned, you fed and walked a dog, and got to sleep with that particular dog next to your bunk."

Sara knew full well the healing power of animals. "Sounds nice." Their fingers brushed when she handed him his water.

For the briefest of seconds, Matt leaned into her touch. "It was."

Still tingling from the casual contact, Sara uncapped

her water, took a sip, then resumed feeding Charley. She needed to hear the rest of the story, as much as Matt needed to tell it. "So what happened to make you feel responsible for Mutt's death?"

Matt gently extricated his palm from Charley's fingers. He looked away a heartrending moment, then took a long drink. "You really want to hear this?" he finally asked.

Her heart went out to him, and again, it was all she could do not to stand up and hug him. "I really do," she answered softly. It was the only way she'd begin to understand him and what he'd been through. The only way he'd begin to heal, too.

Wearily, Matt scrubbed a hand down his face. He seemed reluctant, but began to relate: "I had Mutt that night. He woke up around two in the morning, and he was nosing my hand, signaling he needed to go out."

Made sense.

"It seemed urgent, and I thought it was a routine potty break, so I stumbled out of bed and opened the door to our barracks. Then all hell broke loose."

Sara's heart lurched as she pictured the scene.

Matt shook his head, unable to completely camouflage his grief. "Mutt picked up the scent of whatever he'd heard and bolted away from me at top speed, barking his head off. Woke everyone and all the other dogs up."

Sara could imagine that, too.

Matt jerked in a shuddering breath. "Turned out we had a dozen suicide bombers in the compound, ready to kill us all." His voice caught at the unbearable pain of that memory. "Mutt attacked the closest one, and the guy blew himself up. And Mutt along with him." Briefly, he couldn't go on. His eyes glistened. "Just like that, they were both dead. And a minute or so later, thanks to the swift action of our soldiers," he said hoarsely, "so were all the other enemy combatants."

This time she couldn't resist. Sara reached over to touch his arm, her fingers curving around the hard, thick muscles. "Oh, Matt..." she said, aware it was all she could do not to burst into tears herself.

Her attempt to comfort him, even a little, failed.

His forearm remained stiff, resisting. He shook his head, a faraway look in his eyes. In abject misery, he confessed, "The hell of it is, if I had just been a little more alert, or wary... If I would have had my gun, I would have taken out the bomber before Mutt got to him. But I didn't." He swallowed hard.

Aware her initial instincts not to touch Matt had been on point, Sara dropped her hand and went back to feeding a now sleepy-looking Charley the last of his mashed fruit. At least Matt was talking; she held on to that.

"What about the other dogs?" she asked softly, wanting him to get the rest of the story out, to have that much-needed catharsis. "You said there were no troop injuries..."

His glance still averted, Matt released a breath. "There were some injuries. Shrapnel. None of the other dogs were killed." Hands knotting, he shook his head. "But it could have very easily gone another way," he admitted rawly.

With multiple fatalities of soldiers and canines, Sara thought.

Matt drained the rest of his water. "That incident made me realize my time to be effective was gone." Regret tautening his masculine features, he slanted her a look. "I'd already notified the Army I would be resigning my commission and heading back to the USA when my tour was up. And so, that's what I did."

Sara offered Charley a sippy cup of milk.

"And your family…?" Did the McCabes know even part of what he'd just told her?

Apparently not, from his reaction.

Matt's brows lowered like thunderclouds over his gray-blue eyes. "They know I don't talk about what happened over there."

"Except you just did."

He frowned. "Only because I want you to know. So you'll stop asking me if I can be hands-on with Champ or any other puppy, because I just can't. I don't want that kind of responsibility." His grimace deepened. "Not ever again."

Talk about a textbook case of PTSD. Sighing, she got a washcloth and cleaned Charley's face and hands. Removed his bib.

Matt came closer. His mood shifting, now that his heart-wrenching confession had been made, he gazed gently down at Charley, who was now slamming both his palms happily on the high chair tray. "So I'll gladly write a check. But as for the rest," he gritted out, "there is just no way, Sara."

Sara understood guilt, unwanted memories and unbearable pain. More than he would ever know.

Matt exhaled. Then moved so she had no choice but to look into his eyes. "And I would appreciate it," he said, as their gazes locked, held, "if you didn't talk to anyone else about what I've just told you."

Even if it would help him eventually? Sara wondered, conflicted. Still, she knew a confidence deserved to be kept. So she did what she knew in her heart was right for their friendship, which miraculously seemed to be resuming.

"Okay," she said, letting out a long breath, and lounging against the counter, too. "I won't tell anyone what you went through over there. But if you do want to talk to someone…someday…"

He moved away again, his manner as gruff as his low voice. "No. All I want to do is put it behind me."

Easier said than done, she thought.

But she understood.

Sometimes the only way to get past pain that immense was to stop reliving it and move on. Survive and advance. Hour by hour…day by day.

He removed a checkbook and pen from his shirt pocket.

"So, what do you think it will take to fund a drive for volunteer puppy raisers? Will a thousand dollars be okay to start?" He squinted at the hesitation he saw on her face. "What?"

Noticing Charley was beginning to look very sleepy, she lifted him out of his high chair, walked into the living room and sat down in the rocker glider. She brushed her lips across the top of his head, then positioned him so his chest was cuddled against hers, his head nestled in the crook of her shoulder.

Aware Matt was watching her closely, appearing to feel the same tenderness for her son that she did, she returned. "New ideas, and the money to fund them, are always appreciated."

He followed and settled on the ottoman opposite her. Knees spread, hands clasped in front of him. "But?" he asked quietly.

She smiled ruefully, as Charley sighed and closed his

eyes. "I'll be blunt. I don't think this is going to solve your problem with your family."

Matt frowned. "Why not?"

Since Charley was drowsy enough to put down, she rose and carried him over to the Pack 'n Play in the corner of the breakfast nook. When she'd settled him, she turned back to Matt and said, "Because I know your sister, Lulu, and your mother, and they're going to see *any* extroverted action by you, no matter how small, as a much-needed breakdown of the walls you've put up around you since you came back from the Middle East. And they are going to want to *expand* on that."

Matt frowned. "So their nagging will increase, not decrease. Is that it?"

"Pretty much." She went into the kitchen to put on a pot of coffee.

Arms folded in front of him, Matt lounged against the counter again. "So what do you suggest?"

She shrugged, wishing he didn't fit into her household quite so easily. "It's your family."

He watched her measure coffee into the paper filter. With a wry half smile, he pointed out, "You come from a large family, too, darlin'."

As always, the endearment melted her heart and made her way too aware of him. Physically, and in other ways, too. She poured water into the reservoir.

"Yes, but mine are spread out all over the country now. So their ability to badger me in person is limited mostly to phone calls and texts. They generally don't just show up on my doorstep. Well," she amended hastily at his skeptical expression, "my parents have come to see us a few times, and hinted that I should start looking for a job close to the university where they live and teach in

Colorado Springs. But for now at least they've accepted that I want to raise Charley in the community where Anthony and I grew up."

His glance drifted over her. "Think you will ever change your mind?"

Good question, one she was still wrestling with. "I don't know. Maybe. But I like my job at Healing Meadow Veterinary Hospital. They've been really good about extending my maternity leave past the terms I initially thought I wanted."

Although it had been rough, going through the last six months of her pregnancy alone, after her husband's death. She'd had the support of her work colleagues and other single moms that she knew. Plus, her parents had come to Texas for Charley's birth, and helped her for a few weeks after that, but since then, she had been mostly on her own, with help from friends whenever she needed and or wanted it. Of course, it wasn't the same as going through a pregnancy with a loving husband at her side, sharing every moment of Charley's growth and development with his daddy. Having Matt around today had shown her that. Made her long for an intact nuclear family, and the kind of hope-filled future a situation like that would bring.

Luckily, Matt had no way of knowing how emotional she was feeling, deep down inside.

Still, his attention deepened in a way that warmed her from the inside out. In deference to her sleeping son, he moved slightly closer and kept his voice low. "What terms did you want from your employer?"

She swallowed and tried not to flush. She may have had an unrequited crush on Matt once—when they were teens—but they were destined to be nothing more than friends now.

"Six months."

Turning away, she forced herself to ignore the intense yearning for closeness, and the flutter of desire that swept through her. "But now that Charley is six months old, I can see I'm not quite ready to go back full-time."

Ignoring the masculine warmth and strength emanating from his tall body, she busied herself wiping down the high chair. "So I'm going to stay on leave another three months, and then ease into work by taking emergency calls every other weekend, and seeing patients one day a week."

Matt observed, "And you're taking on Champ, too."

Who, Sara noted, was curled up in a ball in his indoor puppy pen, fast asleep.

"For just a month or so." She hoped, anyway. "But yeah, I really am going to have to find someone to help me with that."

She got out the cream and sugar and set them on the island, along with a plate of oatmeal-cranberry-pecan cookies.

Matt watched her fill two mugs. "What about Charley?"

Their fingers touched as she handed him his mug. Aware she was tingling more now than she had been before, Sara furrowed her brow. "What do you mean?"

"You said you were going to need help to work with Champ and watch your son simultaneously."

Sara stirred in cream and sugar. "Right."

Matt drank his black. "Would you consider letting me assist you with your son?"

Sara paused. Was this guilt talking—or something else? She looked him up and down. "Let me get this straight. You…Mr. Lonesome…want to be Charley's baby wrangler?"

Matt's broad shoulders lifted in an affable shrug. "Why not? He likes hanging out with me. I like hanging out with him." He paused. "Don't trust me?"

Sara blushed. Yet another obstacle to her going back to work. "Actually," she admitted with chagrin, "I don't really trust anyone except for Bess Monroe, and your sister, Lulu, with Charley—if Bess is around to supervise, and I only have confidence in Bess because she's a registered nurse." Which was, on the face of it, pretty neurotic, she knew.

"Ah." Matt dunked the edge of his cookie in his coffee. "New-mom anxiety."

Heat rose in the center of her chest as she waved off her worry. "I know it's silly…"

"But it's the way you feel, darlin'. No shame in that."

Pleased to find him honoring her feelings instead of making fun of them, Sara nodded. "Exactly," she said softly. "Plus, I really don't want to be away from Charley for all the time it's going to take to socialize Champ because then I'd end up feeling I was neglecting him. So it's a real conundrum."

Matt finished off his cookie, understanding again. "How do you formally socialize a puppy, anyway?"

"By introducing him to as many different people and places as possible over the next month. So he'll be comfortable no matter where he is."

"Sounds…interesting."

Sara smiled, suddenly aware how cozy this all felt. With the two of them there, chatting, and the puppy and baby sleeping nearby.

Matt was going to make a wonderful husband and father someday.

Trying not to think about the toe-curling kisses they'd

already shared, she admitted, "The outings would be good for Charley, too. He's spent way too much time at home with just me, thus far. But—" Sara took another sip from her mug "—I can't handle both Champ and Charley out in public by myself." Which meant some sort of accommodations would have to be made.

Again, Matt understood. Practical as always, he asked, "So why don't we do it together, then?"

Chapter Four

Sara stared at Matt, as if sure she hadn't heard right.

He understood her confusion. Because he certainly hadn't expected to make such an offer when he'd come over here, either. But something about being around her and Charley made him want to leave his self-imposed isolation behind.

"You want to help me socialize Champ?" she asked, still appearing stunned.

The thought of having to be in contact with the puppy sent a cold chill down his spine. "No. I still don't want to get that close to any dog." Never mind a sweet, adorable puppy who could easily steal his heart if he allowed it. "I want to take charge of Charley while you train Champ."

Sara slanted him a sideways look. "You understand that I would want us all to go out in public together? You'd have to leave your ranch and come over here, help me load them in my vehicle *every day* for one month, or until Alyssa Barnes is well enough to take over Champ's training and care?"

He figured he could handle that as long as he wasn't in charge of the leash. He nodded, admitting ruefully, "Initially, I figured avoiding dogs entirely was the way to go. But—" he paused to draw another breath "—you've helped me realize that is more apt to provoke questions than avoid them."

Her jade eyes gleamed. "So you're going to take the opposite tact."

He moved forward, hands spread, his voice edgy with tension. "I want to desensitize myself, the way a person would after any trauma."

Sara offered a supportive nod. "Kind of like when you get thrown off a horse. The last thing you want to do is get back on one, but if you don't get back in the saddle as soon as possible, you may not ever be able to ride again."

"Right." The understanding in her eyes encouraged him to dig a little deeper into his feelings. "I'm not planning on falling in love with the pup, or even having much to do with Champ. I just want to be able to be around him and not start thinking about all the things I'd rather not think about."

She looked at him from beneath the fringe of her lashes. "I hear you."

She certainly seemed to. And not just in the way a compassionate woman would, but like someone who had been through her own version of hell.

Matt cleared his throat. Maybe the two of them would be good for each other, after all. "So when and where do you want to start Champ's socialization?" he asked.

She paused. "This evening okay with you?"

* * *

"I know what you're thinking," Sara told Charley several hours later. She rushed around her bedroom, trying to get ready.

"I'm getting awfully dressed up for an outing with you and Champ and Matt, but it isn't a date. Even if it is Saturday night. And it sort of feels like it could be one. It's absolutely not."

Charley gurgled from the seat of his battery-operated swing.

"It's just that the Spring Arts and Crafts Fair at the community center is a pretty big deal around here." Sara paused to put on her favorite gold necklace and matching earrings. "Everyone goes, and everyone gets a little bit dressed up. Usually cotton dresses and cardigans for the ladies, and button-up shirts for the gentlemen. And of course—" she mugged affectionately at her son "—adorably cute outfits for the little ones, like yourself."

Her doorbell rang.

Sara glanced at her watch.

"Oh dear." Matt was early. Charley still wasn't dressed, and Champ still had to go out.

Thanking heaven that she at least had gotten in her favorite yellow dress, Sara finished zipping up the back, then eased Charley out of his swing. Doing her best not to get drool on her dress, she carried him to the front door.

Matt stood on the other side of the portal, looking handsome as could be in a tan button-up shirt and jeans. "You okay?"

"Yes." She inhaled a whiff of his sandalwood-and-leather cologne, noting how closely he had shaved. "Why?"

He shrugged. "You're perspiring."

Okay, it really wasn't a date, she thought in wry relief, because if it had been a date, he would have had more sense than to point that out. She waved an airy hand. "I've been rushing around."

"How can I help?"

With a grin, she drawled, "I was hoping you'd ask." She shifted her baby into his strong arms. "Entertain Charley while I gather his stuff."

"Any particular reason why you chose this event for Champ?" Matt asked.

Sara motioned for Matt to follow her up the stairs to the nursery. She stopped by the master bedroom long enough to grab a pair of soft beige ballet flats. One hand on the door frame, she paused to slip them on. "A couple, actually. First, it's indoors, so it'll be well lit and we don't have to worry about the weather. And secondly, there will be a fair amount of noise and excitement and a ton of people there of all ages."

Matt's gaze shifted upward, from her feet to her face. "So there'll be a lot for both Charley and Champ to take in."

A little embarrassed she had inadvertently just given him a glimpse of her bedroom, post wardrobe crisis, she said, "Yes." Trying not to flush, she reached for Charley and put him on the changing table.

She needn't have worried whether Matt would judge her indecisiveness, though. He seemed to have something else a lot more serious on his mind.

"Are you going to have Champ on a leash?"

Was he nervous about being around the pup himself? Afraid that might trigger some sort of PTSD-like reaction on his part? Worried she couldn't handle the puppy in a crowd and might lose track of Champ? Or just not really looking forward to that part of their excursion? She sighed. There was no way to tell, given the inscrutable look on his face. Although he hadn't reacted to the adorable black Lab puppy's presence thus far with anything more than guarded disinterest.

Figuring the best way to engender calm was to exude it, Sara casually let him in on her plans. "Actually, I'm going to carry Champ in my arms tonight. That way, when he starts meeting a lot of different people, he'll still feel safe. And he won't get tangled up around our feet since he's not that great on a leash yet." Although he would get there.

Matt nodded with what appeared to be relief. "What about this little fella?" he asked.

Sara eased off her son's terry-cloth onesie, changed his diaper, then slid on a blue-and-white playsuit. "I'll adjust the BabyBjörn and you can carry him in that, or you can push him in the stroller. He'll probably be happy either way."

Matt considered. "Might be better to put him in the Björn, so he'll be high enough to really see what's going on."

Sara was delighted Matt had no problem being close to her son. She went to get the canvas carrier, and fifteen minutes later, they were on their way. Matt drove his pickup truck. She drove her SUV, with Charley in his infant seat and Champ safely ensconced in his carrier.

From the looks of the crowded parking lot, the festival was already in full swing when they arrived. Sara put her son in the BabyBjörn and then helped Matt ease it over his shoulders. Charley gurgled with excitement and leaned back against Matt's broad chest. The sight of the two cuddled up together so contentedly was enough to make her swoon. As well as wish that Charley had a daddy like Matt in his life, all over again…

Satisfied all was well, Sara smiled contentedly. She snapped a leash on Champ's collar and led him to the grass. She gave him the appropriate command and the little pup promptly relieved himself, while Matt stood a short distance away.

"Good boy, Champ!" she praised him warmly, since one of the things she was teaching him was to go potty on demand. "Good boy!" She scooped him up and together, she and Matt went into the building where the festival was being held. As expected, Charley got his share of affectionate greetings. Sara was mobbed with people wanting to pet Champ, too.

What Sara didn't expect was to run into Matt's sister, Lulu. The dark-haired honeybee rancher was older than Matt by two years, and to twenty-eight-year old Matt's continued aggravation, had been known to be both bossy and protective of all five of her brothers. As well as stubbornly resistant to *their* advice.

"Hey!" Lulu grinned as she came forward to give them all a hug. Hands on her hips, she stood back to look at Matt. "I knew you were donating funds to recruit new volunteers."

Sara had told Lulu and his mom as much, in order to ease the pressure on Matt.

Lulu's McCabe's blue eyes sparkled. "But I didn't know that she'd talked you into helping out with the puppy raising, too!"

Matt's expression became impatient.

"He's just helping me out with Charley while I socialize Champ," Sara explained.

She realized, too late, she should have added that little

tidbit to her email to both women. She hadn't because she had figured it would mean more if they'd heard about that part of the bargain from Matt.

"Even more interesting," Lulu murmured, waggling her brows.

Matt gave his sister a quelling look. "I don't see how," he retorted.

"Well, for months now you've refused to go out with anyone I've tried to fix you up with!"

Lulu had been trying to fix Matt up?

If so, then why didn't she ask me? Sara wondered, a little jealously, given the fact they were both single, the same age and had known each other before. Then she immediately pushed the ridiculous notion away. She was a widow with a new baby who had also made it clear to everyone around her that she didn't want a love life…

Exuding sisterly exasperation, Lulu continued, "Nor would you deign to ask anyone out on your own! And yet here you are…with Sara and her crew…on what certainly *looks* like a social outing…"

Once again, Sara lifted a staying palm and stepped in to clarify. "Only in the sense that the festival is a community event. And we are all members of the Laramie family."

Lulu looked at Matt, wordlessly beseeching him to verify that was indeed the case.

Instead, to Sara's consternation, the big jerk merely shrugged and kept a poker face. Mulishly refusing to comment either way.

Determined to set the record straight, Sara continued firmly, "If we want Champ to get used to all sorts of crowds and venues, we have to bring him to all sorts of gatherings. Some big, like this. Some medium-sized. Some small and intimate."

"Uh-huh," Lulu said.

Sara flushed. "I know what you're getting at, Lulu, but this is not a date!"

Lulu grinned. Looked from Sara to Matt and back again. "Methinks the lady doth protest too much."

Heat continued flooding Sara's face as she recalled, without wanting to, the kisses she and Matt had shared on his ranch. "We're just friends," she repeated.

"Mmm-hmm." Lulu beamed with excitement. She patted both their arms before she moved off. "Let's see if you two stay that way…"

"You know, you could have helped me out with your sister tonight," Sara said later, when they got back to her ranch and put an exhausted Champ and Charley to bed.

Matt folded his arms across his chest. "You seemed to be doing okay."

"She thinks we're dating!"

The corners of his eyes crinkled. "So?"

"So, we're not!" Sara shot back heatedly.

Mischief glimmered in his gaze. "Okay."

In deference to the sleeping little ones, she kept her voice low and tranquil. "What do you mean, 'okay'?"

He looked her in the eye. "Okay," he replied genially, giving in, "we're not dating."

"But…?" she prodded, sensing there was a lot more going on in that handsome head of his. Emotions she needed to know.

He looked down at her patiently. "It occurred to me that if I help you with Charley every day for the next month or so while you socialize Champ, people are going to see us together. A lot."

As always, his ultramasculine presence made her feel intensely aware of him. Her pulse raced. "Which is why we should make it clear to everyone we're just friends."

Something flickered in his expression, then disappeared. "We can do that."

"But…"

Matt rubbed his hand over his jaw. "People are going to think what they want to think anyway. So why not stay mum and let them jump to whatever conclusion they're going to jump to anyway."

She shivered under his continued scrutiny. "I don't want to pretend that I have feelings for you that I don't have."

He moved toward her, throwing her off her guard once again. "You have to have feelings for someone to go out on a date with him?"

"At least a basic attraction."

The wicked gleam in his eyes said if he thought she would allow it, he would kiss her again.

The trouble was, she knew she would.

"I think we already established we have that," he deadpanned.

She tingled all over, recalling his embrace. Lower still, she felt a melting sensation. Sara swallowed and moved toward the kitchen, picking up a few burping cloths and bibs that needed washing. Her back to him, she took them into the utility room and dropped them into the hamper that held Charley's baby laundry. She turned around to face him again. "I told you those kisses weren't going to happen again."

He moved to let her exit. "I'm not going to lay odds one way or another."

Being alone with him always seemed like a dangerous proposition to her way-too-vulnerable heart. Never more so than now.

Feeling a little overheated, Sara removed her cardigan and draped it over the back of a breakfast room chair. "But you think I am going to kiss you. Eventually."

His smile widened. "Definitely a possibility."

She lounged against the counter and searched for a way to keep them in the just-friends zone. "Look, Matt, I'm not going to lead you or anyone else on. I *don't* want to get married again."

He shrugged and ambled closer, his eyes never leaving hers. "Great, 'cause I don't want to get married, either."

There was no doubt about it. Matt McCabe had to be the most infuriating man ever! Ignoring the skittering of her heart, she tipped her head up, refusing to get sucked in by the blatant sexiness of his gaze. Feeling parched, she went to the fridge and took out a big bottle of sparkling water. "Then what do you want?" she asked.

He watched as she filled two glasses with ice and quartered a lime, already seeming to be mentally making love to her.

"Besides a warm, willing woman to make love with… who doesn't expect any more from me than I want to give?"

Her knees suddenly weakened treacherously, for no reason she could figure. Trying not to fantasize what that would be like, she cleared her throat and prodded, "Besides that."

"Well, then, it'd have to be, for my mother and my sister to stop haranguing me."

Glad to have something else to focus on, Sara worked in the lime wedges and filled their glasses with sparkling water. "Are they badgering you about something else besides the therapy-puppy program?"

Matt nodded tersely. "My mother wants me to participate in the West Texas Warriors Association programs for ex-soldiers returning to civilian life."

So I'm not the only one who senses you're struggling, Sara thought, feeling simultaneously comforted and worried. She handed him a glass and, together, they went into her living room to sit down.

Always ready and willing to lend an empathetic ear, Sara took the sofa. "Why does she want that?"

Matt sat in a big upholstered chair, kitty-corner from her. A faraway look came into his gray-blue eyes as he took a long, thirsty drink. Then let out a ragged breath. "She thinks the only people who will ever be able to truly understand what I saw and experienced while overseas are other military personnel."

As much as Sara tried, she couldn't begin to imagine what he'd been through. Or more important, how he felt now. "Your mom might have a point."

He rested his glass on one muscular thigh. "Did Anthony go to WTWA?"

"No," Sara admitted with heartfelt emotion. "And I wish he had."

"Why?"

Regret tightened her throat. "Because there were times when he was just so remote from me. Kind of shut down and moody, and I didn't know how to deal with that."

Matt's eyes darkened. He took another sip. "You could have just let him be."

Sara nodded. "That's what I ultimately did do."

Matt studied her. "And now you regret it."

"Yes." Sara's voice caught, and the sorrow inside her welled. "Because now he's gone," she confessed, as her vision blurred with tears, "and I'll never know what he was going through, or not going through." Unable to sit still a second longer, she set her glass aside and rose. Moving to the desk, she took a tissue from the box and dabbed her eyes. "Or what I might have done differently to help him reconnect with me."

Suddenly, Matt was behind her. Hands cupping her shoulders gently, he turned her to face him. Threading a hand through her hair, he cupped her cheek and lifted her face to his. "That was his choice, Sara," he said gruffly.

Was it? she wondered, even as she sank into Matt's warm, comforting touch.

The next thing she knew, Matt's other arm was around her waist, bringing her closer still. "I think letting him have his space was a good thing," he said.

As she met Matt's gaze, she could see he really felt she had nothing to regret. Relief flowed through her. Followed by a surprising willingness to let him comfort her.

Maybe she hadn't really done anything wrong.

Or been remiss…

Maybe her late husband's death was part of a larger destiny…one neither she nor Anthony had any control over. As she looked up into Matt's face, she noted *he* seemed to think so.

Aware maybe it was time for her to move on, just a little, she let herself drift toward him a little more.

His other hand slid up, into her hair, and cupped her face as he tenderly murmured her name. Desire sifted through her. And then all was lost as his head lowered, her eyes shut and he fit his lips over hers.

If the first time he had kissed her had brought her back to life…the second time opened up her heart. Simultaneously erasing her need to grieve and heal in private… and keep any future romance from her life.

His kiss was slow. Exploratory. As ever so tenderly, he brought her all the way out of the past, and into the present.

And still he kissed her, inundating her with the heat of him, his masculine strength and tenderness. His tongue tangled with hers, giving as well as taking, persuading, seducing. Slowly, purposely demanding everything she had to give.

Until she kissed him back, hotly, ardently. Her arms were wreathed about his neck, her breasts pressed against his chest and there was nothing but need and more need.

And still the clinch continued, his caresses filling her with everything she had ever wanted and required. Lower still, she felt the depth of his passion. Shivers swept through her. She melted against him, her insides fluttering even as she struggled to keep her feelings in check. He was so hard and strong. The feel of his body pressed up against her sent a maelstrom of ardor pulsing through her, and an even stronger wish to connect with him, heart and soul, woman to man.

But it was too soon for them to search out such intimacy.

They both knew that.

With a sigh of regret, she tore her lips from his.

"We're just supposed to be friends, remember?" she reminded shakily.

"I know." He rested his forehead against hers and released a ragged sigh, revealing himself to be every bit as ripe for a reckless red-hot love affair as she was. He straightened reluctantly. "I'm not going to apologize." Mischief gleamed in his eyes. "But I know what our bargain was…"

It simply wasn't going to deter him in the least.

Which was a problem, Sara thought, as another wave of longing sifted through her. Given how much angst they both still had to grapple with in their personal lives.

With effort, Sara gathered her defenses and looked deep into Matt's eyes. She couldn't help her late husband, true. But she might still be able to help Matt reach out, the way Anthony hadn't. Even if he resented her interference…

Still in the circle of his arms, her hands lightly splayed across his chest, she drew a bolstering breath and firmly and calmly steered the conversation back to what they had been discussing before their embrace. "Is that why you don't want to be involved with the WTWA? Because you're afraid if you do participate in any of their programs, they won't give you your space?"

Expression gruff and forbidding, he let her go, stepped back a pace and told her, "I'm not afraid, darlin'. I just don't have time to join anything until I get the Silver Creek pastures fenced and ready for grazing, since Cullen wants to be able to use them by next fall at the very latest."

Sara knew a fake excuse when she heard one. Matt could call on his four brothers, and his father and sister, and endless McCabe cousins, and get all that done in no time. "You're making the time to help me," she pointed out, refusing to back down with him, the way she had with Anthony.

"Yep." His eyes glittered with something akin to

anger. "And look what that's reaped. Endless questions from you. Matchmaking from Lulu."

She knew he was signaling her to back off, but her heart was telling her to behave differently.

Defiantly, she closed the distance between them. Took his big hand in hers. "I just want you to be happy, Matt." She squeezed his fingers firmly. "After all you've given to our country," she told him, "you deserve it. All our returning warriors do."

He looked down at their joined hands for a long moment, his expression inscrutable. "You mean that?"

His hand felt so warm and strong beneath hers. She looked into his eyes. "Yes," she said huskily, "I do."

His gaze roved her face, lingered on her lips, then returned to her eyes.

"You know what will make me happy?" he finally said.

Another kiss, she thought hopefully, suddenly having second thoughts about the deal they'd made. And becoming aware of the fact that she wouldn't mind someone warm and willing to make love with, too, someone who wouldn't ask her for things she couldn't give, not ever again.

And that would be Matt.

"What?" she returned softly, thinking this was it, the moment he would make his move on her, again. And this time, foolish or not, she would not stop him.

"What do you want from me, Matt?" she asked softly, aware she would do whatever she could to help him come back to life, in the same way she now was.

His mouth took on a harsh, formidable line.

"No more questions."

Chapter Five

Sara realized they needed to take a step back from each other so, for the next week, she arranged to meet Matt at their destinations. It was a little harder, getting both the puppy and her son in the car simultaneously without his help, but it made Champ's training a lot less intimate.

There was little time for them to say much at all to each other as they took the little puppy for thirty-minute visits to the preschool, the pet store, the local farmer's market, an office building that had elevators, and the ladies' auxiliary group at the community chapel.

Matt just strapped on the BabyBjörn and amused Charley while Sara took charge of Champ and his leash.

When they were done, she thanked him, he nodded his acknowledgment, and they went their separate ways.

It was so to the point, in fact, that she was sure they'd be able to get through the rest of the month without getting any closer when, of course, all hell broke loose, and she had one of the worst nights ever as a new mom and temporary puppy trainer.

So, an hour before they were to meet, she called Matt and left a message on his voice mail, telling him that evening's training was off.

Thirty minutes later, her doorbell rang.

Matt was on the other side.

He looked as if he had been in the shower when she called. His hair was still wet and smelled of shampoo, his clothes clean and rumpled. His handsome face etched with concern, he asked, "What's wrong?"

And for once, she had no idea at all how to answer that.

Silence stretched between them. Matt caught the fleeting glimpse of unhappiness in Sara's eyes.

"Nothing," she finally said.

Wary of adding to her distress by saying or doing the wrong thing, he looked down at her. He had never seen her looking so bedraggled. Or fatigued. She had spit-up and drool and what appeared to be baby food smeared over her loose white blouse. Her fair skin was unusually pale, her jade eyes were red and puffy—as if she'd been crying a lot—and her golden-blond hair was escaping from the knot at the nape of her neck, going every which way.

All of which combined to make him wonder what in heaven's name had been going on over here, since he had seen her the previous day.

She'd been completely pulled together, as usual, then.

His heart going out to her, he walked all the way inside and shut the door behind him. Closing the distance between them, he put a comforting arm around her shoulders. "Didn't sound like nothing, darlin'," he pointed out gruffly. In fact, in the recorded message, her voice had been clearly distraught.

She extricated herself deftly and eased away. Spying a soiled disposable diaper on the coffee table, next to the impromptu changing area on the sofa, she picked it up and carried it to the trash. "I didn't get any sleep at all last night."

He could see that, too. If he looked past the puffy redness, he could see the circles beneath her eyes.

Clearly, she'd been through hell.

A second later, he began to realize why when Champ let out a happy bark, did a little leap and then scrambled up and over the three-foot wooden side of the whelping box. Free, and deliriously happy to be so, the puppy came skidding toward the two of them at full blast.

Simultaneously, Charley—who'd been sitting in his high chair—let out a wail.

Sara scooped up Champ before he could head for the foyer staircase. She started to hand Champ off to Matt. Then appeared to abruptly remember their deal. She took care of Champ, he wrangled her baby.

A furiously wiggling Champ in hand, she sent a distressed look back to the now wailing baby. Tears gathering in the corners of her eyes, she sighed and said to Matt, "Would you mind?"

No wonder she was exhausted. And appeared at her wit's end. He would be, too.

"I'm on it." He went over to pick up the still-sobbing Charley. Who stared at him through tear-blurred eyes.

The six-month-old baby looked every bit as tired and stressed out as his mommy.

Only Champ was full of energy. Sara carried the writhing puppy outside and set him down on the grass.

Matt followed, baby in his arms. "Charley teething again?"

Sara made an empathetic face. "No teeth have come through his gums yet, but I think he still is." Her shoulders slumped. "That's not the problem."

Matt moved close enough to inhale the faint scent of lilac clinging to her skin. "Then what is?" he asked, tamping down the urge to take her in his arms and hold her close as she needed to be held right now.

She retorted, "Champ finally figured out how to get out of his pen!" Aware the puppy had finished, she snapped a leash on him and guided him back inside the house.

So he had just witnessed.

Unsure whether it was frustration or fatigue causing her to respond so emotionally, he pointed to the large wire dog cage in the corner of the living room that, so far as he could discern, anyway, had gone unused. "You've got a crate right there," he said, while Charley curled up against him, peering over his shoulder.

"Yes." Sara perched on the back of the sofa, leash still in hand. She looked down at the adorable puppy now resting at her feet, like the perfect little angel he apparently had not been. "And every time I put Champ in that crate, he goes crazy, barking and trying to get out. Which in turn makes Charley start to cry. The more Charley cries, the more Champ barks."

Matt was beginning to see why she appeared so completely wrung out. "And this went on all night?"

She drew a deep bolstering breath, the action lifting the swell of her breasts in a way that reminded him of all the things he was forbidden to do, as per the terms of their bargain. "Yes."

Matt pushed away the yearning to make love to her. One day things could change—in fact, he hoped they would—but right now they had immediate problems to solve. He shifted Charley to his other shoulder. "What are you supposed to do to stop that?" Charley nestled his head in the crook of Matt's neck.

Sara smiled at the way her son was cuddling up to Matt. She came closer, looking a little more tranquil now. "Get Champ used to the crate."

Matt noticed how soft and kissable her bare lips were. Remembering how sweet she tasted, he said, "And you haven't been able to do that so far."

She flexed her shoulders. Linked her hands behind her neck, stretched in a way that made her physical fatigue all the more apparent. "No."

Resolved to help her, Matt mulled all this over. "He's okay when you put him in his little crate in the car."

"I know." She pointed to the airline-style plastic crate she used for travel that was next to the door to the garage. "And I tried putting Champ in that last night and it didn't work, either."

"Why not?"

She huffed out a breath. "Do you think I would be this exhausted if I had figured that out?"

He flashed her a crooked grin. "Sorry. Didn't meant to imply—"

"I'm ineffective?" Sara frowned as more hair fell out of the schoolmarm bun at the nape of her neck. She removed the elastic that had been holding it. Her hair spilled to her shoulders in a golden cloud, and she combed her fingers through it, still voicing her frustration with unchecked emotion. "Well, apparently I am, at least when it comes to training a puppy."

Champ seemed to know he was in trouble. He sighed loudly, and put his chin on his outstretched paws.

Aware this would be a lot easier if there were two adults and one puppy and one baby, Matt continued walking an increasingly drowsy Charley back and forth. "You've never done this before?"

"No." Sara sighed and stared down at the leash in her hands. "My parents didn't allow pets when I was growing up. I didn't have time for an animal when I was in vet school. And when I got married, my husband informed me he didn't really want a pet. So, I never got one."

A fact, Matt noted, that seemed to frustrate and disappoint her.

Sara's soft lips twisted in a self-effacing moue. "I've delivered puppies and kittens and taken care of them in a veterinary medicine setting, but the rest of it is all new to me."

It wasn't like her to just give up on searching for a solution. Unless she was as privately depressed as she seemed to assume he was. "Did you ask the people in charge of the puppy-raising program?"

She looked down her nose at him. "Yes. Of course I asked. They said that I need to leave Champ in the crate until he stops barking and then take him out. Praise him for good behavior. Give him a chance to run around and relieve himself and get some water. And then put him back in. If he barks or otherwise misbehaves, ignore him. When he's quiet, take him out."

Made sense. "Has that worked?"

Sara threw up her hands. "Not so far. He never stops barking, and Charley won't stop crying." Without warning, the tears she'd been holding back streamed down her face.

"Hey," Matt said, wrapping his free arm around her shoulders and pulling her in close, the way a good friend—not a lover—would. "I'm here now. It's going to be okay."

Sara sniffed and buried her face in his shoulder. "I don't see how," she muttered against his shirt.

Deciding the hell with the rules of their baby bargain, Matt ran a hand down her spine, soothing her as best he could with one hand. "I'll supervise Champ, get him to calm down and maybe even sleep for a while, too," he promised, as Charley, alert to the sound of crying, leaned over to look at his mother, perplexed.

"How?" Sara cried, even more distraught.

Matt had always been good at problem solving. "You leave that to me," he told her firmly, then seeing that Charley was about to burst into empathetic tears, said, "Why don't you take Charley upstairs? So both of you can get some rest."

Sara straightened. "It's too late in the day for a nap."

Clearly, Matt didn't think so.

"Dinner will be in another hour..."

"I'll wake you whenever you want." He handed her the baby and took the leash. "Go."

She paused, clearly tempted, yet worried, too. She looked deep into his eyes. "Are you sure you want to take care of Champ?"

"Yes," he said, and found to his amazement, it was true.

There were larger issues at stake right now than what had once been the stuff of his nightmares.

Seeing her doubt, he pointed out, "I've been around Champ all week. And it hasn't been a problem. In fact, it's gotten easier for me every time I've seen him." He squared his shoulders. "This will be another way of getting back in the saddle, so to speak." It didn't mean he had to fall in love with the little pup, or even get emotionally attached.

Sara glanced down at Champ, who was now settled next to Matt's feet, gazing upward adoringly.

She started to relax.

Ready to do what was needed for all concerned, Matt cupped a hand on her shoulder. "Everything down here will be fine," he reassured her gently. "Now go. Sleep. I'll take care of Champ."

Sara woke several hours later to the smell of something delicious—and no barking. Beside her on the king-size bed, a pillow framing either side of him, Charley yawned and stretched. Sara sat up and saw it was seven thirty.

As she'd feared, they were way off schedule. Which wasn't such a problem for her, but it might be for Charley. And Champ...

They would just all have to make-do. Hopefully, with Matt's continued help.

She ran a brush through her hair and put on a clean shirt, then carried Charley to the nursery for a diaper change. When he was changed, they went downstairs to find Matt in the kitchen, the leash attached from the pup's collar to his belt. Champ was lying on the floor beside him, watching Matt intently, the scene so calm and cozy it brought sentimental tears to Sara's eyes. Surreptitiously, she wiped them away. She must still be way over-tired, although she admitted, the nap had done her good.

Matt turned to greet her with a smile. She did her

best to smile back. Gesturing at the slow cooker on her counter, she asked, "What's this?"

His gaze radiated casual affection. "Beef stew. I put it on this morning." He came closer, inundating her with the fragrance of his soap and cologne. "Champ and I took a ride over to the Silver Creek to pick it up while you all were napping. Brought it back and plugged it in here to continue cooking."

Sara put aside the notion of what it might be like to have him here with her like this every evening. As much as she might need and want the help, it wasn't part of their bargain. Hence, it wasn't going to happen.

Ignoring the new skittering of her pulse, she lifted the lid. Saw chunks of beef, potatoes and carrots simmering in a rich, thick gravy. She shook her head in admiration. "Well, it looks and smells amazing."

He grinned proudly. He took a spoon out and scooped up a bite. Blew it softly to cool it, then offered it to her. "It's my mom's recipe."

Sara tasted the delicious entrée. Grinning, she gave him the thumbs-up. "You really cooked this yourself?" she asked. As they stood there, side by side, it was all she could do not to think about kissing him again.

"I did. I like to have something good waiting for me at the end of a long day in the field."

As she met his eyes, a new spiral of warmth slid through her.

"I also brought over half a pecan pie and makings for salad. I figured since I was inviting myself for dinner, I should contribute."

Charley reached out and grabbed the sleeve of Matt's shirt in his small fist. Ignoring the tender look he threw her son, Sara swallowed through the dryness of her throat, and said, "I'll owe you a home-cooked meal, then."

His eyes locked on hers. He responded with lazy pleasure. "I'll take you up on that."

Deciding she had been ensnared in Matt's keen gray-blue gaze for too long, she said, "Mind holding Charley for a minute while I get his dinner ready?"

"My pleasure." Matt shifted the little boy into his arms, grinning as Charley gurgled and patted Matt's broad chest with the flats of both hands.

Sara warmed the chicken and vegetable baby food in the microwave, spooned it into a trisectioned baby dish, and added a little applesauce, too. She nodded at Champ, who was still resting at Matt's feet. "How did you get him to be so quiet and calm?" Since the pup had discovered his ability to be a little escape artist, he'd been brimming with adrenaline and the need for adventure.

Matt shrugged. "Simple. He's really tired. We did some leash training around the yard when we got back."

Sara turned her attention away from the compelling sight of her son snuggling up to Matt. So this man was not just strong and protective, he was amazingly tender, too. So what? That didn't change anything between them. And if she allowed herself to think it would, they'd both be in big, big trouble.

She went to find a bib for Charley. "Thank you. I know this wasn't exactly the bargain we made."

Matt's eyes tracked her every step as she moved around the kitchen. "Deals change. Especially in emergencies."

"As much as I loathe to admit it, this was definitely an emergency."

He soothed her with a look that was sexy and self-assured. "Nothing a little sleep for everyone wouldn't cure."

Sara frowned. "The problem is, how am I going to get Champ to be quiet tonight?"

Matt shrugged. "If you want, I can manage his crate training, too."

Sara paused in the act of filling a sippy cup with milk. "You know how to do that?"

Matt nodded. "None of the strays we'd ever brought in had ever been in a crate, so yeah. I could do it. Take him home with me, if you want."

Sara was tempted. Really tempted to just back out of the commitment she'd made. "Everyone signs a contract when they agree to help raise a puppy. To have Champ anywhere else overnight, I'd have to request formal permission."

Matt's eyes darkened. "Which you'd rather not do."

Sara sighed and admitted ruefully, "This is already embarrassing enough. I'm a veterinarian. I should be able to handle a puppy."

Empathy colored his low tone. "You're also a new mother. Taking care of an unhousebroken puppy and a baby simultaneously is a lot."

Oh no. "Did Champ…?"

"Yep. I found the cleaning supplies. Although," he said, lifting one strong hand, "it's really my fault. I know what happens when they start to sniff and circle. I just wasn't fast enough."

Was there no end to this man's generosity? Now that he had started to rejoin the community, anyway. "Well, thank you," she said softly, realizing that she may have misjudged him completely.

His gaze warmed. "No problem."

Sara measured Champ's food into his dish. She petted his head gently, smiling when he wagged his tail, then set it down in front of him. Straightening, she went over to wash her hands, then took Charley from Matt and settled him in the high chair. *As long as things are suddenly so cozy between us...* "Can I ask you something?"

"Sure." He winked, teasing. "Not sure I'll answer..."

Oh, cowboy, Sara thought as his low husky murmur sent another wave of desire rippling through her. She settled in front of her son and began to feed him. Then turned back to Matt, her demeanor as calm as it was curious.

Once again, their eyes locked. Held.

"Why did you come over here in such a hurry this afternoon?"

Chapter Six

Why did I rush over here this afternoon? Matt asked himself as he got the makings for the salad out of the fridge.

So many reasons...

Darkness had fallen outside, but the kitchen lights cast a warm and cozy glow that made the room feel close and intimate, and Sara look all the prettier.

He let his gaze sift over her, taking in the honey-gold hair falling over her slender shoulders, the subtle rise and fall of her breasts beneath her loose apricot tunic. Refusing to let his gaze go any lower, he said, "You sounded really distraught on the phone when you left the message canceling our plans."

She tilted her head. "So you thought something was wrong."

His gaze lingered briefly on her lush, kissable lips. Returned to her eyes, thinking how relaxed she was now compared to how she had been when he'd arrived. Chuckling, he rolled up his sleeves and walked over to the sink to wash his hands. "Wasn't it?"

She wrinkled her nose and gave him a teasing once-over. "Thank you for coming to our rescue."

He tried not to think about her touching him every place her eyes had been. "That's what we McCabes do." With effort, he tamped down his growing feelings. Flashed her the kind of easy smile he gave all his friends. "Help our neighbors."

"Your family should know about this." He admired how her skinny jeans molded her feminine curves. Damn, but she was sexy. "Why?"

"They wouldn't be so worried about you if they did."

He divided the small package of field greens between two salad bowls. Added a package of slivered almonds and a smattering of fresh raspberries and blackberries. Realizing he'd forgotten to bring anything to dress it with, he paused, hands on his hips. "I love my family, but they need to mind their own damn business."

She lifted a skeptical blond brow. Seeming to read his mind, she got up to get vinaigrette and poppy seed salad dressings out of the fridge. She brushed up against him lightly as she set the bottles down on the counter in front of him. "So they can't be worried about you the way you were worried about me?"

She had a point. Except… "I haven't called them crying."

She blushed. "I wasn't crying."

He gazed down at her, aware it was taking everything he had not to haul her into his arms and kiss her again. And this time he wouldn't be just consoling her. "You definitely sounded like you had been."

She averted her gaze and inhaled a deep breath. Her lower lip quivered slightly, as if she might burst into tears yet again. "How about I take Champ outside while you sit with Charley, and then we can eat?" she asked huskily.

Able to see she needed a moment to collect herself, he nodded. "Sounds good."

Her brief respite outdoors gave him a chance to kick himself in the rear for inadvertently saying the wrong thing to her again. When she and Champ came back in, Charley was still in his high chair. He had finished his applesauce. So Sara gave him a smattering of Cheerios to push around the tray while Sara and Matt enjoyed the dinner he'd prepared.

Keeping the conversation businesslike, he asked, "So what do you want to do about the training opportunity we missed this afternoon?"

"I phoned the Laramie Gardens senior living center before I called you and rescheduled for tomorrow afternoon at four p.m." Sara added butter to a piece of the crusty bread she'd added to the feast. "Do you think you'll be able to do it?"

He nodded.

She took a sip of mint iced tea. "I'd understand if you want the weekend off."

Was she trying to put distance between them, or simply being considerate? Her expression gave no clue. "Are *you* taking the weekend off?" he asked, just as quietly.

"No." A contented smile lit the pretty features of her face. She looked over at her son, then down at Champ, who was snuggled up against her feet. "I want them both out and about every day."

Matt shrugged, beginning to relax again, too. "Then I'll help you every day."

She finished her salad and started on her stew. "Is it getting any easier for you to be around dogs now?"

Yes and no, Matt thought. He still did not want to get emotionally attached to Champ, but he savored the time he spent with Sara and Charley and Champ. Maybe because, in their own way, they'd become a little team.

But there were also still times when he'd be out and he would see an older dog that would remind him of Mutt. And that always led to the mixture of grief and crippling guilt that left him unable to sleep.

Aware Sara was waiting for his answer, but knowing she didn't need to be burdened with his problems when she already had so much on her agenda, he shrugged and said with an accepting smile, "Hey, this is America. Land of the free and the brave—and the pets we love. So if I ever want to be able to go anywhere—" and he did, especially with Sara and crew "—I just have to suck it up and deal. You know?"

"I do." They were both finished eating. Sara looked down at the floor where Champ was curled up, sound asleep. She disengaged the leash from her belt, and rose.

Champ slept on.

Soundlessly, she moved away from him and carried her dishes to the sink. Matt followed, just as stealthily. "It used to bother me to be around married couples," she confessed, her soft lips twisting ruefully. "Or people in love. Or women who were expecting who had their husbands at their sides." She bent over to put their dishes in the dishwasher, inadvertently giving him a nice view of her slender ankles, taut calves and sleek thighs.

She shook her head. "It just made me so acutely aware of everything I'd lost and what I'd been through with Anthony's death."

Matt joined her at the sink. Sensing he wasn't the only one who needed to talk about the most difficult moments of his life, he asked, "Did they ever figure out what happened to cause Anthony's car accident?"

"They definitely know he was going too fast when he came to that bend in the road, and that he missed the turn. But there was no drugs or alcohol involved. He didn't have his phone with him, so he wasn't texting or on a call."

"So it was just a freak accident or a moment of inattention."

Regret flickering in her eyes, Sara dipped her head, admitting, "I asked him to run into town and go to the grocery store for me. So maybe he had his mind on that."

Matt knew the path she was traveling. It wasn't good. He cupped her shoulders. "It wasn't your fault, darlin'. Accidents happen."

She nodded, whether in agreement or to end the conversation he did not know. She cleared her throat. "Dinner was delicious, by the way."

He got the hint. Subject change. Now. He smiled, still wishing he could kiss her, and not have her take it the wrong way. "I'll tell my mom you liked her recipe."

She held up a hand. "Whoa there, cowboy. If you do that, you'll also be telling her the two of us had a dinner together that you cooked."

Matt ran a hand across his jaw. "Hmm. How about that."

She narrowed her gaze. "Still using me to get your family to back off?"

At this point, it would be more accurate to say he was using his family as an excuse to spend time with her... and Charley...and Champ.

But sensing she might not want to ponder that right now, given the convoluted way their renewed friendship had all come about, he merely shrugged. Ready to let things stand as they were, for the moment, anyway. He regarded her curiously. "Is that a problem?"

She shrugged. "Only...possibly...for you."

As much as Sara had enjoyed the pleasure of Matt's company, she knew they still hadn't solved the problem of how to get Champ to stay in his crate. "So how is this going to work again?" she asked Matt as bedtime for the little ones approached.

He took the towels he'd brought in from his truck. They were worn but clean. "We're going to rub these towels over our skin and get our smells on it," he demonstrated as he talked, "and then put them in Champ's wire crate, and then he is going to go in, too."

Sara followed suit, moving the terry cloth across her throat, her hands and forearms.

Champ looked surprised when Matt picked him up, cuddled him briefly, then put him in the wire cage, next to the comfort towels. When the door clicked, he began to bark. Unperturbed, Matt stretched out in front of the crate and slid his fingers through the metal grate.

To Sara's surprise, Champ stopped barking. He lay next to Matt's hand, sniffed, and then with a loud sigh, settled, too. As she watched the two of them interact, Sara couldn't help but drink Matt in, head to toe, in all his masculine glory. His hair had dried in rumpled waves that were both sexy and invitingly touchable, his face closely shaven. Clad in a washed-'til-it-was-soft ivory chamois shirt that stretched across his broad shoulders and muscular chest, and faded jeans that did equally nice things for his hips and legs, he was every inch the indomitable Texan. Ex-soldier. Rancher. Daddy and husband-to be…?

With a sigh, Sara forced herself to stop thinking about what an eligible man Matt was, and how attracted she was to him. Then she asked, "Now what?"

Matt smiled up at her, oblivious to the unexpectedly sensual nature of her thoughts. "We sleep."

Sara blinked. "On the floor?" Yes, there was an area rug, but beneath that it was solid oak. Which would definitely not be comfortable!

Matt's smiled widened. He looked like a cowpoke on a campout. He winked. "Well, not you and Charley, naturally."

Sara went over to give Charley's swing another turn. As her son began to sway again contentedly, she walked back to Matt. Guilt assailed her. "But that won't be comfortable for you!"

He folded his hands behind his head. "I wouldn't say no to a pillow."

She hunkered down next to him, aware there were limits as to what she would ask of him. "Matt…" she cautioned softly, wary of upsetting Champ, who would then upset Charley again.

Matt caught her hand in his and squeezed her fingers tenderly. "Do you trust me, Sara?"

She looked into his gray-blue eyes. The answer to that was easy. "Yes."

He gripped her hand again and continued looking deep into her eyes. "Then trust that I can handle this."

With the situation under control, Sara thanked Matt again, and then took Charley upstairs. She bathed her son and got him ready for bed. Gave him the last bottle for the evening, read him a story, rocked and sang to him, then put him in his crib.

Short minutes later, Charley was sound asleep.

She turned on the baby monitor and eased from the nursery.

As she walked back into the master bedroom, the outside lights clicked on. After slipping the portable monitor into her pocket, she grabbed the items Matt would likely be needing if he were staying the night, and walked back downstairs to investigate.

Matt was standing in the moonlight, watching Champ romp in the grass. He stood, legs braced slightly apart, hands shoved in the pockets of his jeans. Aware the spring night was beginning to get a little chilly, she walked over to join him. Once again, she felt as if she and Matt were leaders of the same team. A family team.

Barely able to comprehend just how comfortable that felt, Sara turned her attention back to the black Lab rollicking in the grass.

Amazed at how easily Matt had taken control of what had seemed to her to be a completely untenable situation, she inclined her head at Champ. "He didn't make a sound, not that I heard."

Matt turned to her, his handsome features bathed in the glow of the lamps above. The corners of his mouth lifted into an amused smile. "Yeah well—" he shrugged his wide shoulders "—he didn't go to sleep, either, but that will come."

Sara bet it would. "I noticed you moved the crate closer to the sofa." Where she had also deposited a pillow, blanket, washcloth and towel, toothbrush and toothpaste.

"As long as he's right next to me, I think he'll be fine."

She studied his profile, deciding he was way too sexy, whatever the time of day or night. Way too capable and masculine and kind as well.

Aware she could fall all too hard for the handsome rancher if she weren't careful, Sara folded her arms in front of herself. "I get that this approach might work tonight…" Who wouldn't feel safe with Matt stretched out beside them?

He turned. Seeming to zero in on her nervousness, he leaned in close, his smile slow and sure. "But…?"

Inhaling the intoxicatingly familiar scent of him, she edged back. "What about tomorrow?" She couldn't help but ask. "Are you doing this so you'll have to spend the night every night?"

"Hmm." He looked over to see her shivering in the night air. "Hadn't thought of that." He wrapped an arm about her shoulders and brought her in close to his side. His eyes gleamed devilishly. "But ah…now that you mention it…" he teased her softly, bending down to whisper in her ear "…the idea does have a certain appeal."

He favored her with a flirtatious smile that did funny things to her insides. And the chase was on.

Sara tried not to think how much she enjoyed having him around, or how easy it would be to start depending on him. Even though their deal was set to go on for only three more weeks. She cleared her throat. "Seriously…"

Matt tightened his arm around her shoulders, in a friendly squeeze, then let her go. All Texas gentleman once again. "Seriously," he said drily, "he will get used to the crate in the next twenty-four hours or so and soon it will feel as cozy and safe to him as your arms."

Relief mixed with the desire starting up inside her. As their glances meshed and held, all Sara could think about was kissing him again. Not that she had any business doing that, either, when he was clearly a man who needed a wife and children, even if he hadn't realized it yet, and her heart was locked up tight. "I don't know how to thank you enough for all your help. I was at my wit's end."

He knit his brows together and teased in a soft, low voice that sent thrills coursing over her body. "Well, there might be a way."

Her heart skittering in her chest, Sara lifted her chin. "And what is that?" she asked, almost ashamed to admit what favors she could think of, off the top of her head.

Smiling, he stepped a little closer to her. "My family is having a potluck at my parents' ranch on Sunday afternoon. Lulu's bringing her Honeybee Ranch food truck which is going to make its debut in downtown Laramie next week. She's going to be testing a couple entrées. Everyone else is bringing sides."

Giving herself a second to recoup, Sara checked on Champ, who was still running circles in the grass. Finally, she turned and hazarded him a glance. "Sounds fun."

"Glad you think so," Matt said, and flashed his most persuasive smile, "because I'd like you to go with me."

"As a friend."

He made a seesawing motion with his hand. "Like I said, we don't have to label it."

Was he trying to confuse her? She stepped closer, too. "But your family will assume it's a date."

His hands settled on his waist. "Possibly."

Talk about infuriating. She lifted a censuring brow. "Or probably?"

"Does it matter?" He studied her for a long moment,

and then his shoulders flexed in an offhand shrug. "You and I will know what it is."

Except, Sara thought, working hard to conceal her traitorous emotions, she really didn't.

She knew what she foolishly wanted it to be…a start to something more…that could lead to either a really close lifelong friendship, the kind where they could lean on and be there for each other, no matter what… Or… they could reach for something even more romantic and fulfilling, that would rid her of her grief and guilt, and ease the physical loneliness she felt. Even if it weren't dating, per se.

Unfortunately, she realized, taking in his casual expression, it did not seem as if she and Matt were on the same page.

He continued, matter-of-factly, "A favor from one friend to another."

As it turned out, Matt was correct. Champ did sleep through the night, and he did not bark again in his crate, so long as Matt was next to him. It was a little odd having the big, strong rancher there in the morning when she and Charley woke up, but as the morning progressed, she got used to the sight of him in rumpled clothing with dark tousled hair and a day's growth of beard. And she knew she could really get used to him making blueberry pancakes for them all and then accompanying her while she took Champ and Charley outside to enjoy the beautiful spring morning.

By the time Matt left to go back to his ranch, to shave and shower and tend to things there, Champ was so tuckered out he went willingly into his crate, curled up next to the old towels that smelled like her and Matt, and fell sound asleep.

The trip to Laramie Gardens went well, too.

"I can stay," Matt said, when they got back.

Wary of getting too dependent on the handsome cowboy, Sara shook her head. "No, I've got it," she said.

And to her satisfaction, she did.

Still, it was nice to see him again the next day when he arrived a little after two in the afternoon to pick them up for the potluck.

She had missed having him around.

And unless she was mistaken, he seemed to have missed being with the three of them, too.

It would have been nice, however, to clarify exactly what this was to him. A date? A return favor for a friend? A simple social occasion between platonic friends?

There was simply no clue on his ruggedly masculine face. Other than the fact that, to her increasing frustration, he absolutely did not want to put a label on whatever this was.

When they arrived at the McCabes' Bar M Ranch for the family dinner, cars and pickup trucks lined the drive. Lulu's Honeybee Ranch food truck was at the end and delicious smells were wafting through the truck's open service windows. They'd barely parked when members of his family started coming up to greet them.

Cullen and his wife, Bridgett, came over to introduce their fifteen-month-old son, Robby, to Charley, and their beagle-mix, Riot, to Champ.

The second oldest of the McCabe brothers—the widowed surgeon, Jack—had his daughters, aged three, four and six in tow. "They want to meet your two fellas," he told Sara drily.

"I told you the baby would be cute!" Lindsay, the oldest, said.

"I think I like the puppy better," Nicole, the middle daughter, exclaimed.

"I like 'em both," Chloe, the youngest, declared.

Sheriff's deputy Dan McCabe and his wife, Shelley, brought over their four-year-old triplets, who promptly knelt to pet both dogs.

"Are you two going to get married?" one asked.

"No!" Sara and Matt said swiftly, while the adults laughed.

"Never say never," Chase McCabe said, as he and his wife, Mitzy, pushed the stroller that held their quadruplets. The two had been sworn enemies, until a business calamity the previous Christmas had brought them together. He wrapped an arm around his wife's shoulders. "We're living proof that miracles can still happen, even in this day and age!"

"I wouldn't mind receiving one," an aproned Lulu said, coming up to join the group.

"Your time will come," Matt's dad, Frank McCabe, predicted warmly. He walked over to welcome Matt and Sara, too. "Don't let them tease you too much," the tall, silver-haired rancher quipped.

Sara smiled back. "I can handle it. What I do need to know is where I should put the strawberry shortcake we brought for the potluck."

Frank directed, "Rachel is setting up a buffet on the screened-in back porch."

Relieved to be away from any of the questions she had a feeling were going to be coming up from the siblings, Sara headed for the rear of the house while Matt and his dad took charge of Charley and Champ.

Matt's mom, Rachel, was indeed on the back porch, setting out a lovely spread of homemade dishes. During the week, in town, the petite dynamo put her silvery blond hair up and wore suits and heels befitting her job as a tax attorney. On weekends, she left her hair down and dressed like a rancher's wife in jeans, boots and feminine cotton blouses. "Where would you like these?" Sara asked, showing Matt's mom what she had.

Rachel smiled. "Over here."

Sara stepped back. "Anything else I can do?"

"If you want to help me finish setting the table I won't say no." Rachel handed over a basket of silverware. "So how have you been?"

"Good," Sara was surprised to admit, even more so since Matt had come into her life.

Rachel went down the row, placing napkins. "How's Matt?"

Sara tensed. "Isn't that a question for him?"

"It would be—if he would ever tell me anything." Rachel paused. "Really, how does he seem to you?"

Torn, Sara hedged, "I'm not sure I can describe…"

"Try."

Finished with the silverware, Sara started putting out the glasses. "He's been very kind and helpful with Charley and Champ…"

Rachel added plates. "The word around town is that you've been seeing each other almost every day."

Sara nodded. "That's true."

Rachel straightened. "Are the two of you dating?"

Heat spread from the center of Sara's chest, into her face. "Matt—and I," Sara added uncomfortably, "would prefer not to put a label on it."

"So, in other words, yes."

Gosh, Rachel was persistent! But then so were most of the McCabes. And most moms, when it came to protecting their offspring.

"So, in other words," Sara corrected, taking an equally persistent and matter-of-fact tact, "Matt and I are re-establishing a friendship we both thought was long over. We're finding we had more in common than we knew." She flashed a friendly smile. "So, it's all good."

Except for one thing…

Figuring as long as they were talking candidly, she could ask a question or two also, Sara moved a little closer and continued, "What I don't get is why you and the rest of the family are so worried about him. I mean, he's as stubborn as he always was, but he seems fine to me." More than fine, actually, given what had happened to him and Mutt.

Rachel sighed. "I guess it's because, until very recently, he had seemed to be spending too much time alone. Not dating anyone. Which in turn made me wonder if he's really over the other military widow he was involved with."

Other military widow? Sara blinked, feeling gob-smacked. "What are you talking about?"

Rachel paused. "You don't know about Janelle?"

Feeling like she'd just taken a blow to the chest, Sara shook her head. "No," she said, just as Matt walked up to the porch, Charley in his arms.

The silence, already really awkward and rife with emotion, turned even more so. A fact Matt was quick to pick up on.

"Really, Mom," he drawled, "meddling already?"

The older woman straightened. "We were just talking."

Matt gave his mother a chastising look. "Well, now

you can stop because Lulu is about ready to start serving the entrées."

Matt turned to Sara with a smile that did not quite reach his eyes. "Lulu is dying to have you try her honey chipotle chicken wings and honey barbecued ribs…so if you're game…"

"I am."

Luckily, there were no more questions about her and Matt's "romance" or lack thereof from anyone else in the McCabe family during the rest of the party.

When they went home, Matt took Champ out for a last outdoor break and some water, while Sara put an equally tuckered out Charley to bed.

When she came down, Champ was snoozing away in his crate, and Matt was standing in the kitchen, waiting to speak with her. "Sorry about my mom. She can't seem to help herself."

A mother herself now, Sara understood the fierce need to protect, so she waved off his concern. "It was fine." Sara began to put some of the leftovers that had been sent home with her in the fridge.

Apparently for Matt, it hadn't been. "What did she say?"

The real question was, what did Matt *not want* Rachel to reveal? Deciding this was an opportunity to satisfy her own curiosity, Sara shot him a commiserating look and said, "Your mom mentioned a military widow named Janelle."

Matt's stoic reaction did not change.

Swallowing, Sara continued, "She seemed to think there was some parallel between your relationship with Janelle, and your renewed friendship with me."

"There isn't."

Silence fell and he offered nothing more.

Not willing to even consider being in a relationship where she was repeatedly shut out emotionally, Sara decided to let it—and consequently, him—go.

"Okay."

Her heart aching, she pivoted away.

He put a hand on her shoulder. Waited until she made a half turn. "That's it?" he demanded curtly. "Just…okay? No more questions?"

Sara drew a deep breath, unwilling to take all the blame for the new tension between them. "You don't like questions," she reminded him, reining in her emotions, too. Even as her skin heated at his gentle touch. "And I don't like having to ask, so…" Deciding it was best they curtail this conversation, she started to show him the door.

He caught her hand. His gray-blue gaze was sober, intent.

"What do you want to know?"

Chapter Seven

Sara turned around. She'd had all evening to think about this, and she knew that if she and Matt were ever to get really close—as close as she wanted them to be—he was going to have to let down his guard a little. "Were you in love with her?"

He released a short, impatient breath. "I thought I was."

She walked into the kitchen and took two cold sports drinks from the fridge. As she handed him one, their fingers brushed and a thrill swept through her. "Are you in love with her now?"

Twisting off the cap, he shook his head.

Surprised how much this meant to her, Sara tensed. "Are you sure?"

He took a long drink, then studied her over the rim of the bottle. The corners of his sensual lips curved up. "You're not going to rest until you hear the whole sad story, are you?"

Why lie? She didn't know why it mattered so much to her, she just knew that it did. Shrugging, she took a drink, too. "Probably not."

He took her by the hand and led her into the living room, settling on the middle of the sofa. Happy he was about to confide in her, she took the place beside him.

He squeezed her hand, letting their clasped palms rest on his thigh. "A year into my last deployment, one of my buddies was killed while out on a mission. I accompanied his body back to Virginia, where his wife and his family resided."

Sara could only imagine how difficult that had been for him.

As Matt continued, his face became etched with grief. "I was a pallbearer. Everyone was as distraught as you might imagine, and after the service, at the gathering back at the house, his widow, Janelle, and I talked a lot. She wanted to know a lot about her husband's last days. If I thought Dirk had been happy and I told her—honestly—that she had meant the world to him."

Matt swallowed and his voice grew hoarse. "When I got back to my unit, I got all the guys to make a video, recounting some of their best memories of Dirk, and I sent it to her and his family.

"They were really happy to have it. Janelle wrote and thanked us. One email led to another." He shrugged. "And pretty soon we were talking regularly. Six months later, when I had a few weeks leave, she met up with me in Italy." He cleared his throat as an indecipherable emotion crossed his face. "And we went from being friends to something more."

"You were serious about her," Sara guessed. They

were sitting so close she could feel the heat emanating from his powerful body.

"Very." Matt's expression turned brooding. "Anyway, one thing led to another, and before we knew it, we were talking about being together when I left the service.

"At first," he admitted, a mixture of regret and self-admonition filling his tone, "the plan was that I would move to Arlington, get a job there when my tour ended. So we could really date." He exhaled. "Then, she decided that even though we'd only been in a relationship a few months, it was silly to pretend we *weren't* going to end up together."

Talk about jumping ahead! Sara thought in surprise. "And you were good with that," she surmised.

"Initially, yeah." Matt nodded curtly, remembering, clearly as caught off guard then as she was now. He shifted toward her, a soul-deep weariness in his eyes. Compassionately, he related, "Janelle was big on advance planning. And I gave her that because I know sometimes when you're dealing with a loss, you just need something in the future to hold on to, in order to keep going."

"Something to give you hope," Sara said softly. That you can actually control.

Matt squeezed her hand, as if glad she understood. "Right. Anyway, Janelle wanted us to share a home together when I did get out of the service, *but* not the one that she had lived in with Dirk, so she put her house on the market, and sold it, and started looking at high-rise condominiums."

"While you were still on active duty overseas?"

"Yes."

Maybe it was Matt's rugged physicality, but Sara couldn't picture him residing happily in the city, any more than she could see him ever sitting at a desk all day. He wasn't really a suit and tie kind of guy. Casually, she asked, "Were you interested in living in a skyscraper?"

"No. And, in fact, I didn't want her to buy *anything* in Virginia with me in mind because I had already purchased the Silver Creek here, and knew that ultimately I wanted to live in Laramie County. She didn't even want to visit Texas. So we started arguing."

"Over email," Sara guessed.

"And via Skype."

"That doesn't sound fun."

"It wasn't." Matt sighed. "Anyway, I tried to put myself in her place."

That sounded like the gallant man she knew.

"I attributed her need to be near her own family and sort of control everything about our future relationship to the sudden, unexpected way she had lost Dirk. So I finally relented and said we'd live wherever she chose, at least for the first few years. Work obligations would likely dictate it after that. I'd keep my ranch—as an investment and a retreat."

"Sounds fair." Sort of…

"And in return, she agreed not to actually purchase anything until we could look at properties together."

"Sounds practical."

He nodded. "When I got out, I went straight to Virginia, instead of Texas, to see her. I just intended to stay a couple weeks. Then I figured we'd travel to Texas to see my family. I wanted her to meet everyone…"

Also reasonable, Sara thought.

"…and at least see the Silver Creek before returning to Virginia to look for work, but that wasn't in her plans. She said there was no time for us to go to Texas to see my family. She'd already set up properties for us to look at, and appointments for me with job recruiters who specialized in placing ex-military in the Washington, DC, area."

That, Sara thought, was incredibly, ridiculously presumptuous. She tried to put together everything she already knew about him. "And this was after your base was attacked and Mutt died." And he had probably needed his family more than ever, even if he hadn't told them what had happened.

"Not too long after, yes."

"And Janelle knew that?" *Knew you were still reeling?*

Again, a terse nod. "We didn't talk a lot about the attack on the compound because of what she'd already been through, losing Dirk and all, but yeah, she had all the details my family didn't."

Which meant they'd been close. "And she still didn't cut you any slack?"

"I didn't expect her to," Matt said gruffly.

But his ex should have been understanding and sympathetic, Sara thought resentfully. She should have wanted Matt to spend time with the rest of the McCabes. She should have wanted to meet them, too. "So what happened next?"

He stood and walked over to the fireplace. "We did what we always did when a conflict arose—we argued. More bitterly than ever. I told her there was no way I was going to work in an office, or be security somewhere. I wasn't sure what I wanted to do at that point, but I did know that I wanted to be outdoors, and that I was perfectly capable of finding my own employment without her help."

Sara joined him at the mantel. "I'm guessing that did not go over well?"

He turned to face her. "Janelle was furious. She said if I wanted to be with her, I was going to have to honor all her demands." Matt shook his head in irritation. "I'd had enough of all the conditions. So we broke up and I came back to Texas."

Sara took his hand and squeezed it. "I'm sorry." It sounded like he had been through hell.

"I'm not." His gaze narrowed. "All that made me realize that an emotional connection and physical chemistry aren't sufficient for any couple."

She breathed in the masculine fragrance of his skin and gazed up at him. "What do you need to be happy?"

He flashed her a roguish grin. "The kind of easy, satisfying relationship all my siblings seem to be getting, the kind my parents have."

Finding his low, husky voice a little too enticing for comfort, she returned, "That's a tall order, cowboy." But an oh-so-delectable one.

He wrapped an arm about her waist and reeled her in to his side, his mouth hovering over hers. "Maybe," he told her huskily, "not as tall as you think."

Sara had been telling herself she'd been exaggerating the impact of their previous kisses.

The practical side of her only wished that was the case!

The moment his lips were on hers, drawing her in, she was as lost in him as ever before.

Sara knew they should slow things down. Get to know each other again a whole lot better before attempting any kind of physical intimacy.

And while that made sense on a purely intellectual level, emotionally she needed him to put the moves on her. Make her feel all woman to his man. Sexy, vibrant and alive.

For months and months now, she had been living in a dark lonely place, her only joys her infant son and the animals she cared for.

Matt made her feel as if she could have more.

Maybe not forever.

Maybe not in any truly meaningful or long lasting way.

But she could have pleasure, she discovered, as his hands slipped beneath the hem of her shirt, caressing her back and better molding her against his hard, muscular planes.

She went up on tiptoe, wreathing her arms about his shoulders, even as he clasped her closer. And still he kissed her, deeply, irrevocably, his lips seducing hers apart and his tongue tangling with hers. She felt the pounding of his heart, the depth of his desire. She tasted the essence that was him.

And still she wanted him.

Wanted *this*.

Matt hadn't intended to let them get any closer than they already were. Hadn't planned to take her in his arms and kiss her again, because it would add a whole host of complications to an already tenuous situation.

She was vulnerable.

So was he.

In different ways, to be sure, but the bottom line was he was not what she needed. And, despite the passion flowing between them, he did not want to take advantage.

But remaining emotionally aloof around her was proving to be a futile task when she melted against him, kissing him back, again and again and again. The blood thundered through him and he reveled in the soft surrender of her body pressed against his.

With a groan, he tore his mouth from hers. Breathing raggedly, he closed his eyes. "If I don't leave now..."

"I know." She kissed his throat.

With another groan, he looked down at her. "Sara..."

She unbuttoned his shirt. "I want you to stay, Matt." Her gaze zeroed on his. She lifted her chin, challenging him to dare to try and chastise her for choosing to live her life anyway she chose. She pressed another kiss on his collarbone, shoulder, jaw. "I want to make love."

He emitted another lust-filled sigh.

Then seeing the raw need, and the fierce determination in her eyes, decided, why fight it?

She was an adult. They both were. And if this was what they needed...

"Upstairs?"

She nodded and took his hand.

There was plenty of time as they made their way to her bedroom to change their minds.

They didn't.

Instead, she drew him over to her bed, then lifted her arms to encircle his shoulders and kissed him with a wildness beyond his most erotic dreams. With her breasts pressed intimately against him, her hands sliding up and down his spine, she rocked against him in a way that had all his gentlemanly instincts fading.

Drunk with pleasure, he undressed her and filled his hands with her lush, delectable curves. She was incredibly beautiful, soft and silky all over, damp with desire.

She stripped off his shirt, dropped her hands to his fly. His jeans came off, then his shorts.

He let her call the shots, let her be in control, until

they were almost there. Then he laid her back on the bed and slid between her thighs.

She gasped as his hand found his way to the feminine heart of her. Shuddered as he helped her find the release she sought. He found a condom. Slid upward. Lifting her to him, easing in, then diving deep. She closed around him like a tight, hot sheath, and together, they soared toward a passionate completion more stunning and fulfilling than anything he had ever felt.

Afterward, they clung together in silence, still shuddering, breathing hard. But as normality returned, so did Sara's usual reserve. To his disappointment, Matt felt the barriers around her heart going right back up.

When she turned on her side, away from him, he bent over to kiss her bare shoulder. "Hey…" he said softly, wanting her to know this was not casual. Not…meaningless.

She waited, not moving.

But how to approach it? In a way that wouldn't insult. "Maybe we should forget about not using labels."

This caught her attention.

She turned back to him, caution in her pretty green eyes. "And do what?" she asked in surprise.

"Date."

Chapter Eight

"Oh, Matt," Sara said wistfully.

She draped the blanket around herself and moved elegantly to her feet.

Regret flowing through him like the tide, he sat up, too, and reached for his boxer-briefs. Damn it all. He had known it was too soon to make love to her. Given what had just happened between them, though, it shouldn't be too soon to ask her out. In fact, that should have happened first. Probably two weeks ago, after the first time they kissed.

"If you're worried about this making things too complicated between us, you needn't be," he said gently, determined to ease her worries and lighten her mood. He sent her a look filled with mischief. "Complicated is just fine with me."

With a low laugh, she shook her head. "Oh, Matt," she said again. The picture of sated elegance, she gathered her bra and panties off the floor. Managed to don her panties with the blanket still around her.

With a faint shake of her head and a soft exhalation of breath, she let the blanket fall all the way to the floor. Giving him a fine view of her curvaceous backside in the process. And though he could no longer see what lay beneath her floral print cotton panties, he remembered the petal softness well.

He felt himself grow hard again.

"Tell me what's on your mind," he encouraged.

Keeping her back to him, she slipped on her bra and fastened it in front. "You don't have to be gallant." She looked at him with weary embarrassment as she pulled her arms through the sleeves of her blouse and shimmied into her denim skirt. "I get what this was." Barefoot, she disappeared into the adjacent bathroom and came out with a brush.

Aware it was just as arousing to watch her dress as it had been to undress her, he shifted on his jeans. Reached for his shirt, too.

"For both of us," she added, suddenly looking a whole lot more practical and a lot less emotional than the situation warranted.

"Hmm." Matt stroked his jaw in a parody of thoughtfulness. "A long time coming, maybe?" he teased.

She nixed his guess. "Rebound sex."

To Matt, that was both good news and bad. Bad in the sense that she put it in the category of something not necessarily to be repeated again. Good in that... He studied the flush in her cheeks and the shimmer of feminine embarrassment in her jade eyes. "You haven't...?"

Her tongue snaked out to wet her lower lip. "Not since Anthony," she confirmed softly. Then demonstrated the kind of mutual interest he hoped she would. Swallowing, she looked him in the eye. "And you?"

He was pleased to report, "Not since Janelle."

He'd thought the fact he didn't bed women recklessly would be of comfort to her.

Instead, it only seemed to confirm what erroneous conclusions she had already made. "See?" She leaned against her dresser, arms folded in front of her, satisfied her point had been made.

Their lovemaking had been rebound sex. Nothing more. Nothing less.

Matt finished getting dressed. Hands spread in a gesture of supplication, he walked toward her. "I hear what you're saying, darlin', but I don't agree."

Her chin lifting, she gave him a challenging look that made him want to ravish her all over again.

"If I just wanted to…um—" he tried to think of a respectful way to put it, and failed "—I could have. As could you."

She uttered a smothered half laugh, then sent her glance heavenward, sighed. "What's your point, cowboy?"

He looked down at her arms, which were still crossed militantly in front of her, and knew he had his work cut out for him.

That did not make him any less intent on persuading her to give him…them…a chance, however.

He took another step closer, and looked deep into her eyes, reiterating gently, "It means, Sara—" he took her resisting body all the way into his arms "—that maybe the fact we chose here and now means something."

As Sara gazed up into Matt's ruggedly handsome face, she wanted to believe that. *So much.*

Especially since she'd had a secret crush on Matt for years that had only faded when she got married. After she lost her husband, and Matt returned to Laramie County, that desire had come roaring back. Hence why it wasn't a surprise to her that they had ended up in bed.

She also knew the night had been an emotional one. For them both. He yearned for the kind of satisfying romantic relationship most of the members of his family had. She did, too. But she also knew that kind of romantic love did not happen on a whim. And what they'd enjoyed just now—satisfying and wonderful as it was—had been wildly, recklessly impulsive. Which was something she had never been.

Sara sighed. She wished he didn't look so damn hot, even in his disheveled state, because it was *not* helping matters. "Look, Matt, I'm not the same person you remember."

She focused on the disbelief in his eyes.

"Why do you think that?" He continued to study her as if trying to figure something out.

Heat gathered in her chest and spread through her throat to her face. She knew she had to be completely honest with him, or even a friendship between them would never work. She knotted her hands in front of her. "Because the last decade has changed me."

He pulled her against him for a sweet and thorough kiss that quickly had her tingling from head to toe. He lifted his head, then swept his hand through her hair. "We're both definitely older and more mature."

She splayed a hand across the center of his chest. "And guarded in ways that the people closest to us don't want to see or accept." Beneath her fingers, she could feel the strong and steady beat of his heart.

"It's like there's this wall," Matt said.

She wet her lips. "Around our hearts."

A contemplative silence fell.

She remained in the circle of his arms. "The thing is, I like having that wall around me," Sara said, appreciating how protected and cared for she felt when she was with him, even though she knew her heart was very much at risk. She lifted her head to look into his eyes.

"I feel like it keeps Charley and me safe."

And while such emotional independence was good for her, it might not be good for him.

And because she cared about Matt, she wanted what was best for him. Always.

The corners of his lips lifted ruefully. "You may have noticed I like to keep my distance from people, too, darlin'." He paused, as if sensing that in this one area they were really in sync. His gaze darkened. "The quiet and solitude…the lack of demands…can bring a lot of peace."

She took his hand and led him through the bedroom doorway, back down the stairs. As they landed on the first floor, well away from the temptations of her bed, she drew a deep breath, confessing, "The thing is, my friends and family keep urging me to open up my heart again, and go back to being my 'old hopelessly romantic self.' But I can't do it. I don't want to be that vulnerable or emotionally dependent on anyone again."

So he needed to know this was as close as they were ever likely to get. She wasn't even sure this was sustainable, given how conflicted she was feeling right now.

"Never mind anyone's wife," he deadpanned.

Were they really talking marriage now? "Or significant other." She didn't want that kind of pressure, to make everything turn out all right.

By the same token, she wasn't promiscuous. So she couldn't just have random one-night stands and feel good about it, because that wasn't the real her, either.

Sara's brows knit together. "Why are you smiling?"

He shrugged and flashed her an indulgent smile. "I just find it ironic…"

"Because?" She went into the kitchen to get something to drink.

He followed beside her. "Weddings were all you ever talked about when we were teenagers."

How well she remembered. Her favorite magazines when she was in high school had been centered on being a bride.

She poured him a tall glass of lemonade and handed it to him. "That's because I thought marriage to the love of your life was the key to living happily ever after." How that dream had crashed. "Now I know it isn't."

He regarded her over the rim of his glass. "Because Anthony died."

She sipped the tart, icy liquid. Waited while it soothed her dry, taut throat. "There's that."

He sat down at the breakfast table. As she started to walk by, he hooked an arm about her waist and drew her down onto his lap. "And what else?"

Sara set her glass on the table beside her. She figured as long as she was baring her soul, she might as well tell Matt about this insufficiency, too. "I don't know if it was me." She let her fingertips dance across the broad plane of his shoulder.

"Or Anthony. Or the fact that we had such a whirlwind romance, and then rushed into marriage before he left for the Middle East. But…" She bit her lip in chagrin.

Matt studied her, as always seeing so much more than she would have preferred. "You weren't happy together?"

Finding it impossible to talk about this when she was so physically close to Matt, Sara stood and paced a distance away. Taking a deep, bolstering breath, she forced herself to continue, as frankly as possible, so he would understand what a very bad bet she was as a life partner. For Anthony, and now for Matt…

"Our reunions while he was in the army were always wildly passionate and then so horribly bittersweet and sad when he had to leave."

She could see Matt understood; he had been through the deployment miseries himself.

Doing her best to suppress the remembered hurt, she swallowed. "Then, when he finally did come back for good, he was just… Our relationship was just…so different. He didn't talk to me anymore." She'd felt like she barely knew him, and vice versa.

"PTSD?"

She stuffed down another wave of pain. "Like you, he said not."

Matt's gaze narrowed. "You think otherwise."

"I don't know." Without warning, Sara found herself blinking back tears. "There were a lot of days he seemed completely fine, happy even." When she had a ray of hope. Enough to want to start a family with him. She shook her head, still struggling to contain the raw emotion welling within her. "Others, where he was drinking too much. Flying off the handle. Taking reckless chances." To the point she had been worried and on edge.

Matt leaned toward her, his forearms on the breakfast table between them. "So when your husband's car went off the road one afternoon, in that freak accident, leaving you alone and pregnant..."

And sad and guilty and so much more.

Matter-of-factly, he surmised, "You decided that was it, as far as ever getting married again went. At least to an ex-soldier."

"Yes." Yet life went on. And she had Charley, and for a while anyway, little Champ. And now, temporarily anyway, Matt...?

She swallowed hard, confessing honestly, "I miss my husband every day and I deeply regret that Charley will never know his father, but—" She paused to corral her emotions and draw an enervating breath. "Being a single mom isn't so bad." Doing her best to look on the bright side, she lifted her arm expansively. "I get a whole king-size bed to myself. Never have to negotiate what's for dinner. Or share the remote."

"I can see the pluses of that," he rasped.

As their eyes met, his filled with heat.

"But you still want to do whatever-this-was-tonight again," Sara guessed.

He stood, all Texas gentleman. All honorable McCabe. "When you're ready." Which he seemed to fully expect her to be one day. "Yeah," he said softly, coming over to kiss her one last, completely thrilling time. "I do."

Matt was out in the field, taking down more fence the next morning when his oldest brother, Cullen, drove across the semi-open field and stopped just short of him.

Matt put down his tools and walked over to greet him. "Hey. What's up?"

Cullen emerged from his pick-up truck. "Thought I'd come out to see how things were going out here." He gazed around Matt's ranch, surveying the progress that had been made. "Pretty slow, from the looks of it."

Sensing a talk he didn't much want to hear coming on, Matt pretended not to understand where this all was headed. "You accusing me of being lazy?"

"Nope. Just impractical and stubborn to a fault is all."

"Thanks, bro."

"You're welcome."

They exchanged grins. "As you know," Cullen continued, serious now, "I've got a lot of calves about to be born and I need a safe place to put them and their mamas until they're weaned. I was hoping to lease pasture here, on the Silver Creek, by next month."

The thought of having cattle trucks in and out, and hired hands disrupting his solitude set Matt on edge. With a sigh, he walked back to pick up some of the debris. He carried it over to the bed of his pick-up truck. With as much patience as he could muster, he reminded, "I told you it would probably be another year. Maybe two before I'd be ready for that."

Cullen nodded. "And I offered to bring some of my men over to speed things up. So you could start making money instead of just spending it."

Matt gathered another half-dozen rusty metal posts. "Thanks. I've got it covered."

Cullen stepped in to help. "You sure?"

Matt considered. He was getting better, thanks to Sara, and Charley, and Champ. He still had a ways to go. "Yep. So maybe you better start looking elsewhere for pasture to lease."

Together, they carried the trash over to the bed of the truck, dumped it on top of the rest.

The awkward silence stretched.

"You know, I may only be half McCabe," Cullen finally said.

That again? Aware he wasn't the only family member who'd had issues, Matt held up a staying hand. "You know you're as much a part of the Rachel and Frank McCabe clan as the rest of us."

"Now, yes," Cullen admitted candidly. "Thanks to some recent revelations, brought about by my lovely wife. But there was a time, when I was sixteen and I first came to live with you-all, when I was just like you are now, little brother."

Matt preened. "Incredibly handsome and charming?"

Cullen guffawed—as Matt meant him to do.

Eventually, the twinkle in Cullen's eyes faded. He got serious again. "I had walls around me a mile high. The way you do now."

Matt didn't need reminding that the war had changed him, and not for the better. He scowled impatiently. "What's your point?"

Cullen shrugged. "Just that it's a lonely way to live." His voice grew rusty. "If it weren't for Bridgett and Robby and Riot, and the unexpected way they came into my life…" He paused to shake his head, his affection for his wife, baby and puppy as clear as the blue Texas sky overhead. "Well, let's just say I would not be anywhere near as gloriously happy as I am now."

Matt knew that. He met Cullen's eyes. "I'm glad you all have each other," he said. And he meant it.

Cullen clapped a brotherly hand on Matt's shoulder. "I want you to have a wife who loves you… *and* a family of your own…complete with kids and a dog, too."

Funny, Matt was feeling the same.

That did not mean it was going to happen.

Not with his limitations and Sara feeling the way she did.

Still, the time they were spending together…their passionate lovemaking…had showed him they could have something incredible.

Something enduring.

And Sara was right.

Their relationship didn't have to necessarily be formal or traditional. With time, they could—and would—fashion an arrangement that worked well for them.

And for now, that was enough, Matt told himself firmly. It was going to have to be.

"How's it going?" Matt asked when Sara let him in later that same day. One thing was certain: the mommy in charge looked extraordinarily beautiful in navy leggings and a long-sleeved blue-and-red-striped shirt. Her hair was swept into a loose sexy knot, and her skin was glowing luminously. It appeared whatever misgivings she'd had about their reckless lovemaking had been put to rest by their long talk and amazing good-night kiss the evening before.

He knew he felt good about it. Then and now.

As if it were the beginning of something magnificent…

"Oh, Matt, you have to see this!" Sara announced happily. She made a sweeping gesture toward the center of the living area. "Charley is attempting to crawl."

Matt followed her out of the foyer and hunkered down beside Sara's son. The infant was lying on his tummy on a play quilt spread across the floor. Soft, cloth infant toys were scattered around him. Some within reach, others purposefully not.

"Go for it, Charley," Sara cheered.

Charley gurgled merrily in response, seeming to understand perfectly what his mommy wanted from him.

Impressed, Matt watched Charley lift his head and all four limbs in the air with astounding athleticism, while his tummy remained flat against the blanket.

"It looks like he's pretending to fly," he said, as Charley "pretend-soared" a little more, making enthusiastic noises all the while, then abruptly ran out of steam and let his limbs collapse around him.

Matt eased the toy Charley was reaching for a little closer. With a grunt and a smile, the baby turned over onto his back and rolled the rest of the way toward it.

When his fingers closed on it, he gurgled happily and lifted it to his mouth.

"Way to go, little man," Matt praised, gently touching his baby-soft cheek.

Charley gurgled happily and kicked some more.

Matt looked over at the whelping pen—which was empty— and the crate. Also empty.

Sara knelt on the other side of the blanket. Her son between them. Noting how quiet it was, Matt looked around some more. "Where's Champ?"

"At the WTWA facility in town, working with one of the trainers. I'm supposed to meet up with them in about an hour."

"Is that why you texted me that I didn't need to set aside time to help you-all out today?" Or was it because they'd made love the night before, and she wanted her space, to further reconsider their plunge into physical intimacy?

Although she was clearly happy to see him, there was no clue on her pretty features as to what else she might currently want from him. At least in the romance department.

Sara looked at him from beneath her lashes. "I don't really need you to go with me to pick Champ up, since there will be plenty of people who can help me get Champ and Charley in the SUV simultaneously. But—" she watched as her son rolled back onto his tummy again and set his sights on another toy "—if you want to tag along, it *might* be fun."

He picked up on her cautious tone. "Might be?"

Abruptly, Sara looked torn. She rose lithely and walked over to the kitchen, where she'd been removing the stems of fresh strawberries. "Alyssa Barnes, the wounded infantry soldier who is going to train Champ, was just transferred to a rehab unit in Laramie, for the rest of her three-week recovery." Sara's voice took on an unexpectedly emotional note. "Her parents are bringing her over to WTWA, and she's going to meet Champ for the first time."

So much for her having her affection for the puppy under lock and key.

Noticing her eyes had taken on a suspiciously moist sheen, Matt gave Charley an affectionate pat, then rose and moved to her side. All the while giving her the chance she needed to compose herself.

Out of the corner of his eye, he watched her pull herself together. Their fingers touched as she handed him a luscious red berry, then took one for herself, too. "They're expecting the meet and greet to really boost Alyssa's morale."

At her invitation, Matt helped himself to another berry. "She's having a hard time?"

Sara nodded, her expression grim. "Numerous surgeries, infection, a lot of setbacks." She handed him another couple of strawberries before putting the bowl back in the fridge. "And she has another grueling three weeks or so of PT to go before she'll be well enough to work with Champ completely on her own. But her sister and parents have all pledged to help with that while she's on the mend. So there's no doubt she'll get there."

"When will you be turning Champ over to her?"

"We've set the date for the reunion picnic."

So Sara still had time to come to terms with the good-bye to little Champ.

As did he…

Deciding they needed something else to focus on, Matt observed, "The strawberries are great, by the way."

Sara laid a hand over her heart. "The first real bounty of spring, at least in my view!" She sighed, happy color coming into her cheeks. "I love it when they're sweet. And tart, too."

Unable to resist, he teased, "Kind of like you?"

"Whoa there, cowboy." She splayed her hands across the center of his chest, blushing for a completely different reason now. "Laying on the charm a little thick today, don't you think?"

He smirked in response.

If that was her not-so-subtle way of telling him to stop flirting, he wasn't making any promises. Paternal instincts kicking in, he turned to check on Charley. The little boy was lying on his back, contentedly inspecting a stuffed toy in his hands.

Satisfied they had time to banter, he turned back to Sara. Let his gaze drift over her lazily. "What else do you like in the spring?"

"In terms of fresh produce?" she asked, deliberately

misunderstanding what he was asking. "Pretty much everything…"

"So," he drawled back, "the way to your heart is definitely via your taste buds."

He could handle that. He eased his hand through the wisps of hair at the nape of her neck.

She gasped as he rained a few kisses over the soft, feminine slope of her throat. "Very funny."

Not enough? "A few hot, sexy kisses, then." He gathered her close.

Sara groaned. "Matt…" She used her splayed hands to put pressure on his chest.

Much more of this playing around and he'd be wanting to make love to her, here and now. "Okay." He let her go reluctantly. "But just for the record," he said with a wink, "I'm available whenever…and wherever, darlin'."

His mischievous attitude had replaced the heavy drama of the night before, just as he had hoped. Sara looked happy again. Turned on. Almost carefree…

"Oh, I think you've made that pretty clear, cowboy." Sara responded with a candor he hadn't dared expect.

He noticed she wasn't saying yes, exactly. Nor was she saying no. But they were definitely in "maybe, when the time is right again" territory.

He could definitely deal with that.

She drew a bolstering breath. "In the meantime, it's time for us to go. We've got a schedule to keep."

"OMG! This little guy is so cute!" Alyssa Barnes said as she sat and cuddled Champ in her arms.

Champ, never one to turn away any adoration, licked the red-haired former army sergeant under the chin.

Alyssa looked at Sara, her freckled face alight with

joy. "Thank you for stepping in temporarily so I'll still be able to join the program as planned and help train this little guy."

"No problem." Sara smiled. "You should thank Matt, too. He's also lent a hand."

Alyssa looked at Charley, who was cuddled up as snugly in Matt's arms as Champ was in hers. "Is this your little boy?" she asked the two of them.

Sara wasn't surprised she'd made that assumption. Matt cared for her little boy with all the love and tenderness of a Super Dad. "Charley is my son," Sara clarified.

"Oh." Alyssa looked taken aback, and no wonder, given the affection flowing between the two. It wasn't just Matt who was completely besotted. Charley snuggled up to Matt with total adoration, too. "I thought..." she stammered.

Sara cut her off with a relaxed lift of her hand. "We're just friends." *Although, part of me would like to be so much more...*

"Right." Alyssa paused. Her brow furrowed. She looked down at the black Lab in her arms. "Is it okay if I spend a little more time with Champ?"

Sara looked at Alyssa and her sister, who was there to assist since the former soldier was still in a knee brace, moving stiffly. "Take your time." She and Matt left them in the group meeting room and shut the door behind them.

"Sara? Matt?" Hope Winslow-Lockhart, the director of WTWA public relations, strode toward them. Elegantly dressed as always, the tall blonde executive asked, "Could I have a word with the two of you?"

"Sure," Sara and Matt said in unison.

They walked down the hall and moved into Hope's office.

She gestured for them both to take a seat. "I wanted to update Matt about the progress we are making with the volunteer recruitment initiative, so he'll know how his very generous donation is being spent."

She logged on to her computer and showed them both the new social media page that had been set up.

"We want to add videos of all the people who help teach each service, therapy or companion dog. We're going to use Star—Champ's mother—and compile the video we already have of her during her pregnancy and the birth of her litter, to the very first eight weeks of her nine puppies' lives, while they were all still at Sara's ranch. And then get film of every person working with every puppy after they left the litter. We want to show how the aptitude of each dog is evaluated and let everyone know that in this case it really does take a village to train a dog.

"So, if we could get someone—say Matt—to film Sara on his phone, as she works with Champ, it would be really great."

"I can do that," Matt said.

If he did, it would mean they would be spending even more time together, Sara thought with surprising happiness.

"And of course we'll get film of Alyssa Barnes as she bonds with Champ, too."

"What do we do with the videos?" Matt asked.

Hope handed over a paper. "Just email it to the editor's address. She'll take it from there." The PR director reached for another page. "I also wanted to let you both know that we've got a couple new support groups starting next week."

Her expression sobered slightly. "One for widows and widowers of military personnel."

Sara leaned forward slightly, not sure she'd heard right.

Hope continued, "The other group is for ex-soldiers who are transitioning back to civilian life."

Matt looked about as happy as she felt. "Tell me my family didn't put you up to this," he said brusquely.

Expression tranquil, Hope shook her head. "I was just hoping you both might choose to participate."

"I'm doing okay," Sara said, still feeling a little rattled at having been singled out this way.

Hope smiled. "I know that," she said with her trademark gentleness. "It's why I thought you might be a good role model for the new widows."

Sara drew a breath. Was it stuffy in here or what? All she knew was she suddenly felt slightly claustrophobic. Needing fresh air, she rose. "I don't feel like I'm quite there yet."

Hope stood, too. "Then you could show the others what it's like to be midway point in your recovery," she suggested candidly.

Sara caught a glimpse of Matt's stone face, and forced a smile. "Thanks for the invitation," she said, flashing a polite but firm smile, "but I am too busy with Champ and Charley right now to even consider taking on anything else."

Hope managed not to look disappointed. "Maybe later?"

"I'll definitely think about it," Sara fibbed. Even though she knew she wouldn't.

Hope turned to look at Matt.

Not surprisingly, he merely stood and said, "Sorry. Not my thing."

An hour later, Matt drove Sara, Charley and Champ home. They woke Charley getting him out of his car seat, which he was not happy about. And when Sara sat down to feed her son his dinner, he was even crankier.

"Think it's his teeth?" Matt asked, when Charley refused both his baby food and bottle.

Aware she had just been wondering the same thing, Sara looked in his mouth. The lower gum was pink, and a little more swollen than it had been earlier. "Maybe."

She got out the numbing cream. And a teething ring from the freezer. Charley accepted the first, and batted the second away.

Meanwhile, little Champ—who hadn't seemed to miss Sara and Matt at all while visiting with Alyssa and her sister—chowed down on his puppy food with enthusiasm.

Deciding her son wasn't liable to eat or drink anything until he was in a better frame of mind, Sara took him out of his high chair and, humming softly, danced him around the kitchen.

The movement was enough to make him stop crying.

Matt watched, smiling. "You're really good with him."

High praise from a noted source. Sara smiled back, glad she had opted to invite him to stay on for a while longer. Which he had oh-so-willingly accepted. The fact was, she needed Matt near her tonight. "So are you."

He cleared his throat. "Sorry Alyssa Barnes thought…"

Sara waved his unnecessary words away. "I'm not. It was an easy mistake to make."

Eyes darkening with indecipherable emotion, Matt continued, "I'd be incredibly happy if Charley were my son."

So would I, Sara thought.

She waited.

The disloyalty she expected never came. Wondering if she *should* feel guilty, she frowned.

Matt studied her.

"Does Hope ask you to join a support group a lot?" he asked.

Ah. She'd been wondering if he would bring that up. Though, like her, he didn't really want to seem to talk about it. "This was the first time."

He sauntered closer, his expression curious. "Did it upset you?"

Good question. Initially, she'd felt shocked, almost insulted. Then scared of what taking a step like that would bring.

Aware Matt was waiting for her answer, and that this was a very raw subject for him, too, she chose her words carefully. "I don't want to start moving backward. I worry that dwelling on my loss in a support group, week after week, would lead me to do just that. And that would be bad for me and for Charley, and really, anyone close to me." It seemed to her that Anthony's death had hurt enough already.

Matt nodded. He took her hand in his, gave it a heartfelt squeeze. "Now you know how I feel," he said.

"About joining a group where you're forced to share your feelings with everyone?"

He nodded. "It's not that I mind talking about what's going on with me, privately, from time to time, when it seems appropriate. Or when I just need to vent."

He drew her slightly closer, and Sara tightened her fingers in his, loving the solid masculine warmth of him.

"But making 'true confessions' isn't something I can do on demand," he finished gruffly.

Sara sighed and rested her head on his shoulder. "Me, either."

Another silence fell, more companionable this time. With a soft sigh, she lifted her head. Their eyes locked, and as she gazed into his eyes, she couldn't help but think how right it felt, being with him. Whenever, wherever…

She smiled as her next idea hit. "Maybe we can be each other's support-person," she said.

Matt bent his head and kissed her tenderly, once and then again. "I'd like that," he said.

As he gathered her close, Sara knew she would, too. Even though she still wasn't certain when—or even if— they would make love again. Or be anything more than increasingly good friends.

Chapter Nine

Sara glanced at the clock for what seemed like the hundredth time in the past half hour. Charley cooed from his seat in the windup swing while Champ watched patiently from inside his crate.

"It's weird, isn't it?" she said, checking her cell phone to make sure the battery was fully charged. It was. "Matt is usually so punctual. Early even." He was never late for Champ's training sessions. And he hadn't said anything about missing this one before he'd left last night.

Although, she admitted to herself, it was possible he'd been distracted by the intimate conversation and the kisses they'd shared…and had simply forgotten to tell her about an impending scheduling conflict.

"But there are innumerable reasons why he could have been held up, too," she told her young audience, as she twisted her hair into a knot on the back of her head and secured it there with a couple of pins.

This was definitely not the same situation as the day Anthony never came back from the store. Although, she admitted to herself anxiously, it sure felt like it. Worse, she'd put some dinner on, in hopes that Matt might stay after they were done. A sign she was beginning to care too much?

Luckily, she had no more time to ruminate on it.

The sound of a pickup truck in her driveway signaled she had company. She moved to the front door and heaved a sigh of relief when she saw Matt climbing out from behind the wheel. With a friendly lift of his hand, he strode toward her.

As he neared her, she saw the shadows beneath his gray-blue eyes. His hair was wet, his handsome jaw clean-shaven except for one strip of beard along his jaw where he had missed. "Sorry," he said gruffly, as he moved in close to give her a friendly hug hello, inundating her with the brisk, masculine scent of him. "Time got away from me."

Sara smiled with a mixture of happiness and relief as she nestled against the hard, unyielding muscles of his chest. "Take a breath, cowboy," she teased, still tingling all over when he let her go. "It's all good. Although, I have to ask… Are you okay?"

His brow crinkled in surprise. "Yeah, why?"

Might as well be honest. Blushing beneath the appreciation in his gaze, she ushered him across the entry and into the main living area of her home. "You look like you haven't slept in a couple of days."

He tilted his head in acknowledgment, looking as if he wanted nothing more than to make love to her again, then shrugged. "A lovesick cow kept me up all night."

She squinted back at him, not sure whether he was joking or not. "Seriously?"

He cast fond looks at their two young charges, then turned his attention back to her, tipping the brim of an imaginary hat. Obviously enjoying how flustered she'd become, he gave her a cocky grin. "Yes, ma'am. Had a three-year-old Brahma stumble onto my property in the middle of night, bellowing at the top of her lungs." His lazy grin widened. "I had to catch her and put her in the barn, then look at the brand and the ear tag and figure out who she belonged to."

Although cattle did occasionally get loose, the timing of the escape could have been a whole lot better, Sara thought. Even as the large-animal veterinarian in her wanted to know, "Was the cow okay?"

"Physically, she was fine," Matt reported soberly. "I'm not sure her heart was all that great." He strolled closer, recalling with a smile. "She was in heat. In search of a bull down the road."

Now it was beginning to make sense. "At Chance Lockhart's ranch, Bullhaven, where there are dozens of prime bulls," Sara guessed, trying not to think how right it felt, having Matt here with her this way.

"Yep," he related. "But my unexpected visitor was not a cow meant to breed rodeo stock, so she was out of luck." He shook his head, chuckling. "Not that this deterred her, given the raging state of her hormones. Anyway, she never let up her bellowing all night." Mischief lit his sexy smile as he locked eyes with Sara. He took her hand and pressed it comically over the left side of his chest. "The heart wants what the heart wants, I guess."

Sara's sure did. Fingers tingling at the brief contact, she stepped back and propped her hands on her hips, surveying him. "If you didn't look so tired, McCabe, this would be funny."

"Actually," he said and shoved a hand through his hair, setting the damp strands to right, chuckling all the more, "it's still kind of funny. Anyway, I talked to her owner around dawn and he came to get his lovesick cow around eight this morning."

Sara could imagine what a relief that had been. "Were you able to go back to bed?" she asked before she could stop herself.

His sleep habits were really none of her business.

And she *really* didn't need to imagine him naked between the sheets of his bed. Or wonder what it would be like to be there with him…

Oblivious to the unprecedentedly ardent direction of her thoughts, Matt gave another negative shake of the head. "I had to deliver a big load of mesquite to a barbecue restaurant chain in San Antonio. Just got back a little while ago from that. Went to shower, and here I am. A little late…"

Which explained his wet, shampoo-smelling hair and soap-scented skin.

"…but ready to go." He pulled out his phone. "So want to get started on teaching Champ the sit-stay command?"

Figuring the more on task they were, the better, Sara smiled. "Let's do it."

Luckily, Charley had nodded off in the battery-operated swing while they were talking. Hence, Matt's only responsibility was manning the video camera on his cell phone while Sara put Champ through his paces.

"Okay, Champ, sit," Sara commanded.

The puppy settled on his haunches, while looking up at her.

"Good sit!" Sara praised warmly, giving him a treat. She lifted her hand in a halting manner. "Now stay." Understanding, Champ remained where he was.

"Good boy!" Sara crooned, while Matt looked on proudly, too. "Good stay!" She treated the pup again as he looked up at her intently. And on they went. Practicing walking on a leash, by Sara's side, without pulling ahead or to the side. Sitting and staying longer. Sitting and staying with lots of warm praise and no treats.

Champ aced it all. And like the magnificent helper he was, Matt captured it all on video on his cell phone. When they'd finished, he promptly emailed it in to the puppy-training group at WTWA.

Aware how much she was going to miss these evenings together when their bargain inevitably ended, Sara asked, "Would you mind sending me one, too? I'd really like to have it."

"No problem," Matt said with a genial smile, doing that, too.

Sara gave Champ food and water and put him back in his crate to rest. Charley was waking up from his little nap, so she lifted him out of his swing, handed him to Matt, and then began preparing her son's dinner of baby food, too.

A supremely contented look on his face, Matt held Charley in his arms while lounging against the kitchen counter. Watching them, Sara couldn't help but think what a great daddy he was going to make some day. Probably husband, too. He was such a natural on the domestic front.

It was too bad she wasn't interested in getting married again.

Unaware of the romantic nature of her thoughts, Matt surveyed her thoughtfully. "Is it going to bother you to have to give Champ up at the end of the month?"

Tingling everywhere his glance had touched, and especially everywhere it hadn't, Sara shook her head. With effort, she drew on a skill she had learned in vet school. "I know this is only temporary so I'm making sure I keep my professional distance and don't get too attached."

Although he looked skeptical, as if wondering if that could actually be done with a puppy as cute as little Champ, Matt reached over to grab a tissue and dabbed some drool from Charley's chin. "That's good."

Matt shot Champ, who was now snuggled up against the grate drowsily watching everything that was going on, a gentle look. "What about Champ?" Without warning, he sounded a little worried. "Is the pup going to have a hard time leaving you?"

Wasn't that just the five-million-dollar question.

Sara exhaled. She lifted her gaze to his, answering carefully. "If it were just Champ and me and Charley all the time for a month, and this home was all he knew, he likely would, at least for a short while."

She held up a hand before Matt could interrupt.

"That's why we're getting him used to all sorts of different situations and places and people. To help prepare him for the extensive training and varied experience he's going to have over the next two years."

Matt nodded approvingly, although he still looked a little apprehensive. "He is a pretty calm and outgoing little fella."

Smiling, Sara reflected, "He's definitely got the heart

of a service animal. Plus, he seems to automatically sense where he is needed…as was demonstrated when he met Alyssa Barnes and some of the other soldiers at WTWA." She released a breath. "So, as long as there is a soul in need of comforting, or a wounded vet in need of assistance, I think he's going to rise to the challenge and be just fine. And I know he will be loved, wherever he goes, by whomever he is with."

Matt seemed to trust her assessment. "Good to hear," he said gruffly.

Wondering if Matt were beginning to get a little too attached to the pup-in-training, despite his previous aversion to all dogs, Sara reached for Charley and settled him in his high chair.

Turning back to Matt, she asked casually, as if she hadn't been hoping this would be the case all along, "Would you like to stay for dinner?"

There were a lot of reasons why he should decline, Matt thought. The first being the reason he had been unable to sleep the night before, even before the lovesick cow showed up.

His first visit to the West Texas Warriors Association facility had been as difficult as he'd expected. Seeing the veterans who'd been getting rehab in the glass-walled physical therapy center stop what they were doing long enough to greet Champ warmly had brought up a lot of memories. Good and bad. And though he hadn't had any more nightmares since he had started helping out Sara, Charley and Champ, he had feared he might be thrust right back into the darkness if he did go to sleep. Which in turn had made him wonder if he was doing the right thing in spending so much time with them, given Sara's ever-present need to move on to a happier, trauma-free life. So, aside from the few kisses they'd shared the night before, at the evening's end, he was putting the brakes on the sexual part of their relationship, too.

At least for now.

Until he was sure he could be what she wanted and needed…even in an untraditional, non-married, sense.

"I mean I do owe you a meal, and then some," Sara continued, an uncertain smile curving her soft lips.

Damn. The last thing he wanted to do was hurt her feelings. And given how delicious whatever she was cooking smelled…he'd be a fool to turn it down. Pushing the troublesome thoughts away, Matt straightened. "Love to, darlin'," he said. Maybe this was just what he needed. Maybe *Sara* was just what he needed. "What can I do to help?"

Relief showed in her slender frame and a smile lit up her face. "Finish feeding Charley for me?"

Their hands brushed as she handed him the dish of baby applesauce and some sort of meat and vegetable entrée. Aware all over again how silky her skin felt, it sparked in him a fierce longing to rediscover every glorious inch of her soft, womanly curves. Matt released a rough breath as he pulled up a chair in front of the infant. "I think we can handle that."

Charley watched him raptly, seemingly as happy to have Matt there for dinner as Matt was to be with them. He could so get used to this. In fact, he had a suspicion they all could. "So how has your day been?" he asked Sara, over his shoulder.

As she moved about the kitchen gracefully, he admired how pretty she looked in her yellow button-up blouse, knee-length denim skirt and brown leather moccasins. "Very busy. Since plans are underway for the WTWA service-dog reunion."

"Oh, that's right." Matt shifted his chair so he could see her, and Charley, too. "You're having it at the Blue Vista?"

"Yes. We're having it here at my ranch." Pleasure teased the corners of her lips. "I've got plenty of room. Anyway, I volunteered to help send out the invitations and gather the RSVPs this year, so whenever Charlie and Champ were down for a nap I was busy doing that."

Matt watched Sara put together roast chicken sandwiches on fresh-baked wheat bread, with slices of tomato, red onion, and colby-jack cheese. She added chipotle mayo, then slid them onto the panini press. "Am I on the invite list?"

She looked up, her expression inscrutable. "Did you want to be?"

Two weeks ago he would have said hell no. Two days ago, after making love to Sara, he would have said hell yes. Now…after visiting the WTWA with her…he was on the fence.

To go and be around all his fellow soldiers and the dogs they loved could mean triggering a new slate of hellacious memories. However, to not go would be signaling to Sara that she—and the dog she was training—weren't important to him.

Assuming his answer was no, Sara turned away from him and kept her poker face. She removed the sandwiches from the panini press and slid them onto a plate. "I'd like to have you here," she said gently, "but it's not required. Not by a long shot."

Actually, Matt thought, it was. Especially if he didn't want some other ex-soldier making a move on her. Because whether Sara realized it or not, something was happening with her, too. Her heart was opening up again to new people, new experiences. Same as his.

"I'll not only attend," he promised, reaching over to briefly touch her hand as she put the plates on the table, then returned to the stove to get the rest of the meal. "I'll help out in any way I can."

Sara couldn't say she was surprised that Matt had volunteered once again. The McCabes were gallant to the core.

There had been a moment there, however, before he had accepted her invitation, when she'd sensed something troubling him again.

That worried her.

It was moments like that, when she didn't know what was going on with him emotionally, that had destroyed her marriage to Anthony. She didn't want a similar exclusion wrecking her rekindled friendship with Matt.

Thankfully, he looked okay—albeit still a little tired—now. And maybe that's all his hesitation had been, she thought. The fact he was feeling tired and overwhelmed after a very long day.

Bolstered by the positive turn in her thoughts, she ladled chicken tortilla soup into bowls, set them on a tray, along with the condiments, and carried it to the table.

As she sat down opposite him, he regarded her with interest. "So how is this event usually set up?" he asked, adding shredded cheese, sour cream, pico de gallo and guacamole to his fragrant soup.

"It's very casual. We set up on the lawn. All the attendees bring food and outdoor folding chairs. A couple of people usually man the grills. Mostly, people sit around and share stories, and meet each other's service animals, and at the end of the reunion, we take some pictures."

"How many people attend?"

Sara stirred condiments into her soup. "Last year it was around two hundred. I think we're on track to do about fifty more than that this year. And, of course," she said, tilting her head, "we have invited all the people who have expressed an interest in volunteering in our puppy training program, too. So it could be about 275 total, I think." She smiled at Matt, glad he was going to be joining them. "We probably won't know for sure until the day of, since not everyone RSVPs."

"Can you handle that many people here?"

Matt looked out the window. Dusk was falling, but they could still see the rolling green lawn that surrounded her ranch house.

Sara nodded. "As long as the weather is nice, we can absolutely accommodate everyone. If it's not," she frowned, relating, "then we have to move it to the WTWA building, which can hold that many people and their dogs at one time. Although it won't be as cozy, since they'll be scattered over three floors and a covered outdoor area."

Matt paused, taking it all in. "Let's hope for nice weather, then…"

They talked a little more.

Sara noticed that Charley was chewing on his hand, as if his gums were bothering him again, so she brought out a teething ring from the freezer and handed it to him.

Matt laughed as Charley promptly stuck it in his mouth and rubbed it back and forth across his gum. "Got to hand it to the little guy," Matt claimed, as proud as any father. "He figured out what makes him feel better right away."

Sara nodded.

Like Matt, her son preferred being self-sufficient. As did she, actually. Until now…

Now it was nice having Matt around to help, keep her company and make her feel like a whole lot more might be possible in life again.

She looked at his empty sandwich plate and soup bowl. "What about you, cowboy?" she asked. "Can I get you anything else?"

He shook his head.

"No, but it was delicious."

"Thank you."

Silence fell.

As the awkward pause drew out, Sara looked from Matt to Charley and back again. It was hard to tell who was losing steam faster now that they'd eaten. She smiled at Matt. "I was going to ask you if you wanted to hang around while I made an apple crumble for dessert…but I'm thinking I should offer you a mug of really strong coffee, then send you home instead."

"Both sound really good, don't they, Charley?"

Her son kicked his legs in response and then leaned over and reached for Matt, batting his forearm persistently.

Matt turned to slant Sara a questioning look.

"I think he wants you to hold him," she explained. The really funny thing was, Sara wanted Matt to hold her, too…

By the time Sara had the dessert in the oven, Charley's head was drooping over Matt's shoulder. Sara glanced at the clock, belatedly realizing, "Oh, honey, it's past your bedtime."

Charley offered her a drowsy smile.

"Anything I can do?" Matt asked, still looking a little ragged around the edges himself.

Sara glanced at the puppy still sound asleep in his crate and shook her head. She gestured expansively toward the sofa. "Just have a seat and keep an ear out for the timer on the oven."

Matt offered her a mock salute. "Will do."

Charley's bedtime routine of bath, storybook and bottle took about twenty minutes. When she'd finished, she eased her sleepy son into his crib and kissed him goodnight.

Wondering how Matt was faring, she went back downstairs. Found him with his eyes closed and his head resting on the back of the sofa cushion, his breathing deep and even. Long jean-clad legs sprawled out in front of him, brawny arms folded across his chest, he looked incredibly solid and masculine.

Not sure what to do—leave him be and let him spend the night—or wake him and send him on his way, she edged closer still.

And that was when he stirred, his eyes opening to look up into hers.

Matt blinked. Scrubbed a hand over his face. Groaned. "I nodded off, didn't I?"

"It's fine."

"No. It's not." His voice was a low sexy rumble in his broad chest. Appearing upset with himself, he shifted, moving his weight forward on the sofa cushion.

Her heart going out to him, she moved closer still. And that was when she saw the ugly red wound on the inside of his palm. "Oh my God, Matt," she gasped. "What is that?"

Chapter Ten

Matt got up from the sofa. "It's just a splinter," he said, folding his arms against the hard muscles of his chest and shrugging off her attempt to look at it.

Sara moved in and took his hand anyway, turned it over so she could see. Damn, that was an angry-looking wound. "Did you do this today?"

He shrugged nonchalantly, then lifted his eyes to meet hers. Their gazes clashed as surely as their wills. His scowl deepening, he admitted, "This morning. I was in a hurry. Didn't bother to put on my work gloves."

A wave of concern rushed through her. Followed by a surge of emotion that was even harder to rein in. Still holding his gaze with effort, she fought back a sigh. "You know when the skin around it starts to get red like this, that it's getting infected?"

"I'm going to take care of it."

She dropped her hand. "Really?" Beginning to realize why he hadn't already done so, she challenged softly, "How? Given the fact the splinter is in your right palm and you're right-handed."

He cocked his head. Unable to argue with her assertion, finally said, "My brother Jack's a surgeon."

She nodded, amenable. "You could definitely drive into town and let him take care of it. Or—" she paused to let the sheer practicality of her offer sink in "—you could let me remove it."

His eyes flashed, and another jolt of awareness swept through Sara. Reminding her just how very much she still desired him.

"Or I could just let it be until it's convenient."

Sara thought about the complications that could ensue. Like sepsis.

Determined to help him, whether he wanted her to or not, she stepped closer and curved her hand over the flexed muscles of his bicep. "Not a good idea," she persisted.

He exhaled wearily.

Suddenly she was lumped in with all the other meddling, overprotective members of his family. And though she wasn't eager to become a nuisance to him, she also couldn't knowingly let him walk out of there without caring for him, with the same kindness and concern he'd been bestowing on her.

The oven timer went off.

Glad for the respite from their stare-down, Sara pulled the apple crumble out of the oven and set it on the stove top to cool. Giving Matt no chance to argue further, she went into the adjacent room, came back with a black bag in one hand, a first-aid kit in the other.

A surgeon was a surgeon, after all.

And if she could help…

When she breezed back in, she could see he had made up his mind to cooperate with her. Whether because it was easier than arguing with her, or the splinter hurt as much as she imagined and he really did want it removed, macho attitude aside.

Not that it mattered to her, since she wouldn't have been able to bid him adieu without the gnawing guilt that she hadn't been as neighborly to him as she should have been.

He watched as she inched on a pair of sterile gloves. Then leaned toward her and joked, "I thought you only worked on large animals."

Refusing to let him ruffle her, she narrowed her gaze. "Exactly."

He couldn't help it; he laughed. "Yeah, well, just so you know," he returned, as sexual chemistry arced between them, hotter than ever, "I'm only letting you do this because I still want some of that dessert."

The practical side of her believed that. The apple crumble did smell good.

Almost as good as he did.

"Mmm-hmm." With practiced efficiency and a poker face, she tore open a packet of antiseptic and cleaned the surface of his wound.

Although no sissy, he grimaced and hissed when she touched the skin.

She could see why. The thick jagged splinter was really in deep. Sympathy reigned. What was it about men that made them feel they had to conceal anything that might be conceived as a weakness? "Has this been hurting this bad all day?"

His expression remained impassive.

Sara retrieved a packet of sterile stainless-steel instruments from her bag. "Why didn't you tell me when you got here?"

"I was already late." He shrugged his broad shoulders. "And it wasn't anything you or anyone else needed to worry about."

She glanced sideways at him, then returned her attention to the foreign object needing to be removed. "Stubborn and self-sufficient!"

He chuckled again. "Hey…" He looked her up and down with lazy male confidence. "Look who's talking!"

She flushed despite herself. "I'm a mom." She focused on making a narrow incision in the top layer of skin. "I have to be competent in all areas of my life."

He watched her use the tweezers to deftly remove the wood. "Well, so do ex-soldiers and ranch owners."

"Touché." Smiling, she coated the area with an antibiotic cream from her home first aid kit. "There. All better." She put on a bandage. Started to move away.

He caught her by the elbow.

A shiver moved through her.

"Thank you," he said sincerely.

As their eyes met, emotion shimmered between them.

"You have to take care of yourself," she said, suddenly afraid he wasn't.

He threaded a hand through her hair, his expression gentling all the more. "What I really want to do," he confessed, his mouth lowering to hers, "is take care of you."

Sara wanted that, too.

So very much…

The next thing she knew, she was all the way in his arms. They were kissing and touching in one long sensual line. Her body responded with a lightning bolt of desire, and now that he was deepening the kiss, another more powerful wave had started to surge. Followed by a riptide of longing and suppressed need, an aching awareness of just how alone she had been.

He tasted so incredibly good, she realized. Felt so strong and so right. She groaned as his hands cupped her breasts, his thumbs rubbing across the crests. She curled against him. She had never wanted someone so completely. Or felt so wanted in return.

Matt lifted his head. "You better tell me to leave," he warned gruffly, "if you don't want me to make love to you again."

She laughed shakily. Determined to keep this light and easy and sexy. "Actually, I do. And you should…"

Matt laughed wickedly, as Sara hoped he would. He lifted her in his strong arms and settled her on the island. His gaze still holding hers, he caught her around the middle, guiding her legs snugly around his waist. He reached inside her shirt, undoing the clasp of her bra. She shuddered in anticipation. Smiling, he molded her soft curves with the palms of his hands, then bent his head and kissed her again, deeply, evocatively, until her heart was racing and she was tingling all over.

And still their mouths mated.

She shifted her hips, encountering rock solid hardness, heat. His hands moved to the bare skin of her thighs, and her skirt hiked up, nearly to her waist.

"You feel so good," he whispered, leaving a trail of fevered kisses across her jaw, down her neck. She quivered as his caressing palms went even higher. Then lower. Easing beneath elastic. Finding the feminine heart of her with butterfly caresses. Slow. Deliberate. Determined to help her find release.

She shuddered again, so close to heaven. "Oh, Matt," she whispered, arching with need, "you feel so good, too."

His gray-blue eyes darkened with pleasure.

She shuddered and he coaxed her to respond even more, to let all her inhibitions float away. Until her body pulsed and she tightened her legs around his waist and melted against him.

She had time to draw a breath, and then his mouth was on hers again, hot and hard, and they were kissing as if the world were going to end. She lost her panties. He lost his jeans.

Her nipples budded. The skin between her thighs grew slick once more. She opened herself up to him, longing for the ultimate closeness. He found a condom; she sheathed him. He gripped her bottom and stroked her where their bodies met. And still they kissed. Taking their time. Building their pleasure, pacing their move-ments, propelling each other to the very depths. Until there was no more holding back. They were racing to the very edge, soaring, climaxing, then ever so slowly coming back down.

Sara didn't want the moment to end.

And neither did Matt.

Holding each other. Touching…loving…kissing… They moved upstairs to her bedroom and started all over again. The second time they made love to each other that night was even more thrilling. Sara let her head rest on his chest and she fell asleep, wrapped in Matt's arms.

And woke alone, at midnight. To the sound of Champ whining impatiently.

Sara threw on a robe and went down to let Champ out. To her aching disappointment, Matt was gone. His coffee and their dessert left untouched.

* * *

Sara spent the rest of the night and the morning wondering and worrying. She didn't know why Matt had left without a word to her. Not even a note. She only knew that on some level it really bothered her because it was just too reminiscent of the way her marriage to Anthony had deteriorated before his death.

For so many reasons, she had done nothing about her husband's mysteriously distant behavior.

But she could do something about this.

Even if it was to only find out for certain what was going on with Matt, and by extension, them. So she gathered her courage, called her friend Bess Monroe, and asked the rehab nurse if she could come out and sit for Champ and Charley for a few hours while she went out.

Bess, who was still single and had a raging case of baby fever, was delighted to help out.

Her friend looked over the instructions Sara had written out. "When will you be back?"

"Not sure. An hour, maybe two." How long did it take to get answers and then recover and restore her pride? "But I'll have my cell phone with me."

"No worries." Bess paused, then lifted a thoughtful brow. "Are you okay?"

Well, no, actually... Sara flushed and turned away from her friend's probing gaze. "Why?"

"You look like you haven't slept."

A malady that seems to be going around. Sara collected her phone and keys, and slid them into her bag. "Charley is teething," she said, although that was not what had kept her awake.

"Ah," Bess sympathized. "Well, have fun."

Sara smiled. *Will I? Or will this be something else I'll come to regret?* "You, too."

It only took ten minutes to drive to Matt's ranch. As she drove through the gates of the Silver Creek, she couldn't help but notice the progress he was making these days, clearing the land and taking down aging fence. He had mowed some of the pastureland, too, which gave it a neater, more manicured appearance.

Maybe there was a method to his solitary endeavors, she thought. Certainly, no one could argue with the effort he was making to turn his land into a thriving enterprise.

She found him about a mile or so back from the road. He was working on fence today. Wearing jeans and a tight black T-shirt that showed off how fit and taut his tall body was.

Surprised to see her, he lifted a hand in greeting and strode toward her, wary concern on his handsome face. The brim of his hat shaded his eyes. "Everything okay?"

She ambled close enough to see the darker rim of his gray-blue eyes. "I'm not sure." She rocked back on the heels of her Western work boots and drawled, "Did I do or say something wrong last night?"

His eyes widened in consternation. He surveyed her slowly, head to toe, as if he found her completely irresistible. "What do you mean?"

Trying not to think how attracted she was to him, too, Sara wrinkled her nose. "The way you left. Without a word." *Or a kiss goodbye.*

He flashed a too casual smile. "You were so sound asleep. I didn't want to wake you."

I wouldn't have minded. "Is that all it was?"

Something akin to guilt and regret moved across his

face. He paused. Like he wanted to say something but didn't know how. The moment passed without revelation.

"What else could it be?" he finally said in return.

"That's just it." Sara shrugged in escalating frustration. She knew he'd been hurt, and was wary of making another mistake of the heart, too. "I'm not sure."

Abruptly, Matt looked as impatient as she felt. Their eyes locked for a breath-stealing moment. "I thought I was doing the right thing, quietly letting myself out. Avoiding doing anything that would have seemed…presumptuous."

Given the fact they had just rekindled their friendship, and were keeping things casual, he had a point.

He folded his arms across his chest. "I'm not sure what your rules are, or would be, even if we were dating."

"Which we aren't," she added tartly. Which was another problem.

"So…" He continued to study her, rocking forward. "I'm not sure why you're so unhappy."

Because I feel shut out and abandoned. Even though technically I have no right to feel that way.

Her humiliation and embarrassment increasing by leaps and bounds, she forced herself to behave like the mature adult she was. "You're right," she acknowledged with a heartfelt sigh. "There was absolutely nothing wrong with what you did last night." *Even though I really wish our evening together ended differently.*

She swallowed around the dryness in her throat.

"I'm not sure why I'm so upset," she blurted out reluctantly, aware their passionate coupling had left her feeling way too hormonal. When he continued watching her, as if perplexed, she threw up a hand, adding, "It's not like we're in love or anything."

His brow lifted in surprise and his hands fell to his sides. "Do you want to be?"

To her shock, Sara realized the answer to that was yes.

But not with just anyone. With Matt. And honestly, how crazy, how unforgivably reckless, was that?

Deciding to exit before she made an even bigger idiot of herself, she lifted her hand. "I've got to go."

"Sara…"

She spun around and began hurriedly walking away. "I just came over to tell you there's no need to come to my ranch this evening," she said over her shoulder. "Bess Monroe is going to help me with Champ's training."

He caught up with her in six long strides. "Wait!" He put a gentle hand on her shoulder, staying her forward progress, then moved around so she had no choice but to look at him. "Are you sure?"

That was the hell of it, Sara thought, looking into his mesmerizing gray-blue eyes. She wasn't sure at all. Not of what had happened between them. Of what she wanted. Or especially what he felt.

All she knew was that there were times when she felt incredibly close to Matt. And others when there was an emotional wall between them higher than any she had ever felt with her late husband.

And that wasn't good.

Not at all.

"Yes," she said, forcing one last completely fake smile. For both their sakes, she had to be a heck of a lot more cautious. "I am."

Chapter Eleven

Matt didn't come over that evening, nor did he call.

Or respond to the text message she sent him the following day telling him that he wouldn't be needed to help her with Charley and Champ that night, either.

And while she expected that he appreciated the break from the daily baby and puppy duties, she also sort of expected that he—like her—would be missing the time they usually spent together.

Apparently, he didn't.

And Sara was still trying to figure out what to make of that at six o'clock that evening when her doorbell rang.

Matt was on her doorstep, with Lulu and their mutual friend Bess Monroe flanking either side of him. He looked incredibly handsome in a charcoal suede blazer, starched blue dress shirt and dark jeans. His dress boots were shined to perfection, and since he was holding his stone-colored hat against the center of his chest, she could see that he had gotten a haircut. He'd also done a very nice job shaving. A sandalwood and leather fragrance clung to his jaw, stirring her senses all the more.

Sara blinked. "What's going on?" she asked.

Grinning, Lulu breezed in. "My baby brother has finally come to his senses, that's what! He's taking you on a date!"

Bess waltzed in after her. "To help make that happen, he enlisted our help. We're baby and puppy sitting for you!"

Sara's jaw dropped. Talk about presumptuous! After leaving her hanging, wondering about whatever he was thinking and feeling after their falling out, for nearly two whole days!

Temper rising, she jammed her hands on her hips. Tilting her chin, she formed an officious smile. "I hate to break it to you, cowboy, but it's customary to *call* and ask a woman if she would *like* to go out with you, before you make these kinds of arrangements."

He flashed a sexy grin. "Thought about it." His eyes sparkled the way they always did when he got under her skin. He ambled a little closer, purposefully invading her space. "Figured you'd say no...so I decided to take matters into my own hands."

Sensing fireworks, Bess and Lulu eased away. Sara scowled, even as her heart panged in her chest, trying to think about what it would be like to kiss him again.

Which, after the way he'd left her two nights before, was definitely *not* going to happen. Not ever again!

She glowered at him, letting him know that it was going to take more than a simple dinner out to make things right between them. "You know," she snapped, "you are not the only one around here who does not like to be told what to do!"

His laughter was throaty and implacable. "Figured. Did not dissuade me in the least."

Sara shut her eyes briefly and rubbed at the tension in her temples. She thought she'd felt ridiculously off-kilter before he arrived. Now with him here standing next to her, his big imposing body taking up all the space, she didn't know whether to ignore her hurt pride and forgive him, or do what she'd decided to do earlier, and keep her heart safe and him at bay.

It was pretty clear, however, as he gave her a slow, thorough once-over, what he wanted to do. End their tiff—and all the rules and non-rules they'd set up thus far—by kissing her senseless.

"Don't argue with the man," Lulu admonished.

Ever the romantic, who never seemed to have a boyfriend of her own, Bess chimed in, "I'll help you get ready!" Giving her no chance to argue, she steered Sara up the stairs.

Figuring she could use a temporary respite from Matt's seductive presence, Sara went along docilely. But her mute cooperation ended the moment they entered her bedroom and shut the door behind them. "Listen." She whirled on her longtime friend. "I appreciate you and Lulu trying to help, but I don't view Matt like you two seem to think."

Not since he sneaked out in the middle of the night, and then defended his actions in a way she'd been unable to argue with, at least on a practical level.

Lulu paused. "Not boyfriend material?"

Given how easily he could break my heart? "Definitely not," Sara said.

Bess shrugged. "So kick him out. The three of us will have a gals' night."

While that would have been a wonderful idea two weeks ago, now Sara hesitated.

Bess grinned. "Just what I thought." She wagged a teasing finger. "You can deny it all you want, girlfriend, but you're crushing on Matt every bit as much as he's crushing on you."

Oh heck, why deny it? Especially when he was there, looking so fine. It wasn't like either Bess or Lulu would believe it anyway.

Bess gave Sara an encouraging hug. "Give him a chance." She shook her head in exasperation. "Do you know what I'd give to have a man look at me the way he just looked at you?"

Probably the same thing I'd give, Sara thought. *Everything*.

She sighed, conceding, "Okay, but we're not staying out late." For both their sakes, she was going to insist they be more cautious than they had been. *What was it they said? Slow and steady wins the race?*

Bess waved an airy hand. "Whatever." She disappeared into Sara's closet. "Although if you're home by midnight," she called over her shoulder, "I'm going to be really surprised."

Sara took half an hour getting dressed, and the wait was well worth it, Matt noted happily. The red sheath molded to her slender curves, while the knee-length hem and sleek alligator heels worked together to draw attention to her showgirl-perfect legs. She'd put her hair up in a loose twist at the back of her head. Tendrils escaped, slanting provocatively across her forehead and the nape of her neck.

Resisting the urge to haul her close and press a string of kisses up the slope of her throat, he said thickly, "Wow."

She shook her head at him, but not before he tracked the softness of her lips and the flush in her cheeks.

Lulu and Bess elbowed each other, mugging. "She does clean up pretty good," Bess teased.

Sara gave her friends The Look. "Okay, you two."

She turned to give them instructions on Charley's and Champ's care for the evening. Then, giving Matt a cautious glance, said, "Ready?"

He held the door for her. "Absolutely."

"So where are we going?" she asked, her expression inscrutable.

Lamenting the fact he had almost blown the only real chance he'd ever had with her, he took her by the arm and led her outside to his pickup truck.

"The Laramie River Inn outside of San Angelo." It was the best place for a gourmet dinner in a one hundred mile radius. He'd had to do some mighty fine persuading to get a reservation on such short notice, even if it was a weeknight.

She lifted a delicate brow. "You must really be trying to impress me."

He opened the passenger door. "Or make up with you," he ventured.

She pivoted and challenged him with a gaze that was sexy, self-assured and faintly baiting. "That's really not necessary," she said softly.

He figured he'd be the judge of that.

She put her right shoe on the running board of the

truck and gripped the handle just above the door. He caught a whiff of her lilac scent, even as his attention drifted lower, to the snug fit of her dress across her delectable hips. Oblivious to his arousal, she slipped into the passenger seat with admirable grace.

He waited until she'd fastened her seat belt, then shut her door and circled around to climb behind the wheel. Figuring the more intimate conversation could wait until he had her full attention, and she had his, he said, "So, what's new on the home front? How were Charley and Champ today?"

While they drove, she filled him in on their antics. He told him about the lovesick cow that had showed up on his property again.

A companionable time later, they arrived at the inn.

A private table near the window, overlooking a field of Texas bluebonnets and Indian paintbrush wildflowers, was waiting for them.

Showtime, he thought. He held the chair for her and she slid into it. The next few minutes passed in silence, as they studied their menus, placed their orders and agreed on a bottle of wine. When their waiter left, she looked wary again and he couldn't blame her. He had been a horse's ass and then some.

Matt reached across the table and took her hand. Regret lashed through him. "I'm sorry," he said quietly, forcing himself to be the gentleman he had been raised to be. "There are no excuses for the way I behaved the other night." He might not have been able to sleep there, but… He swallowed around the tension in his throat, finished soberly, "I should have treated you better."

Her chin lifted indignantly. Clearly, an apology was not what she wanted from him. Then what was?

"We went through this, Matt."

Not well, he thought, because the outcome of their conversation had left her studiously avoiding him.

Determined to set their relationship to rights, he covered her hand with his. "Our friendship is important, Sara," he reminded her, savoring the silky warmth of her skin. "More than that, it's good to have you in my life again after all these years apart."

Finally, a chink in her emotional armor.

She released a slow breath, his honesty engendering hers. With a reluctant smile, she admitted, "It's been good to have you in mine." She paused to survey him with slowly building mischief. "I remember you as a kid. It's been nice to get to know you as a grown-up."

He nodded, thinking of all the ways they had both changed, and still likely would. "You, too," he said gruffly.

They fell silent as their first course was delivered.

When the waiter left, he leaned toward her. "Look, I know you don't want to get married again. You made that clear." He forced himself to be honest in a way he hadn't been with anyone else. "The truth is, I'm probably not husband material, either."

For a moment, Sara didn't move. Then something like disappointment flickered in the jade depths of her eyes. "I don't know how you can say that," she returned finally.

He watched her drag her fork idly through her salad. "Because it's true. My time overseas changed me."

She discounted his declaration with a shrug. "Things... like Anthony's death...have changed me, too."

He knew that. He figured it was why she was so scared, so ready to run at even the slightest disagreement or disappointment.

They could still work this out.

They *would* work this out.

"Then we're on the same page," he told her seriously. "Because I want to stay close with you. Not lose track with each other the way we did before we each left for college. So whatever you want. If you prefer us to be just friends," he vowed, even as his body ached to make love to her again. "Or friends with benefits." His voice dropped a husky notch. "Or something in between, you can have it." He paused to let his words sink in. "All you have to do is tell me what would make you happy."

Sara didn't know what she'd expected when Matt had shown up to take her out on a date.

She definitely hadn't expected him to be so direct, or to chivalrously offer her heart's desire to her, whatever that turned out to be.

He leaned toward her. "Tell me I haven't upset you again."

"No." The truth was he couldn't offend her anew. Because she hadn't stopped being conflicted and confused about their relationship.

One minute she was crushing on him so hard she thought she might actually be falling in love with him. The next she was exasperated beyond belief.

"Do you want to make love again?" he asked, his gaze drifting slowly over her face, before returning to her eyes. "Or go back to simply being friends?"

A shiver of anticipation went through her.

Did she want to make love with him again?

The answer was yes. Definitely yes.

Did she want to wake up alone afterward again?

The answer to that was definitely no.

She did want to spend time with him. Every day. Maybe even every night.

And that could lead to trouble, she knew. Because if she allowed herself to open up her heart again and fall all the way in love with him—and he couldn't love her that way in return—it was going to devastate her.

"Sara?" he prodded softly, reaching across the table to take her hand in his.

He deserved an answer. And an honest one at that.

"I'm not sure what I want my future to hold," she said finally, looking down at their clasped hands. Except she didn't want to be hurt again. Didn't ever want to feel she'd been emotionally shut out and abandoned. Or that she had let someone down by not being what they needed and wanted, either. Because that kind of grief and guilt was not something she could handle again, either.

Matt regarded her patiently. "I get that," he replied gently, understanding—perhaps even sharing—that sentiment.

Sara drew a deep breath. *What was it she'd been telling herself? Slow and steady wins the race? Especially when the most important thing of all was keeping Matt in her life.*

Aware it might be better to ask for too little rather than too much, at least right now, she worked up her courage, looked him right in the eye, and said, "So how about we go back to just being friends?"

To Sara's relief, Matt took her request in stride. It was almost as if he had expected that the incredible fireworks they'd shared had been too good too last. That the risks they were on the verge of taking were not going to be worthwhile, after all.

He was in agreement with her. Their top priority had to be preserving what they already knew they could have, a deep and lasting man-woman friendship. And though it stung a little to find he shared her ambivalence, she couldn't blame him.

Life had not been particularly kind to either of them in the romance department. To expect that everything would magically work out between the two of them, after reconciling their friendship and impulsively taking it to the next level, was not realistic at all.

And as a single mom now, she absolutely had to be practical.

So, for right now anyway, friendship was definitely the better option.

At least that was what she kept telling herself as the next week passed, without so much as a lingering look, touch or kiss from Matt.

Oh, they still spent plenty of time together when she was training and socializing Champ, and Matt helped out by simultaneously taking care of Charley for her as they all went through their paces, but that was pretty much it.

They didn't share meals.

They didn't exchange confidences.

They didn't do anything that would lead to further intimacy of any kind.

And while it was a relief on one level, it was also incredibly disappointing on another.

She hadn't expected to ever have sex with anyone else after Anthony died. Hadn't even been able to imagine it. So to find out that she could still want someone had been astounding. And to feel wanted in return had been even sweeter.

She also knew if she had to choose between a lifelong

platonic friendship with Matt and a fleeting love affair, she would definitely choose the companionship.

So this was definitely the better option.

Especially when she could still share certain elements of the rest of her life with Matt.

"You'll never guess what happened overnight!" she exclaimed, when he met her for Saturday's late-afternoon training session.

He ambled in. The spring day was a little chilly, and he looked as ruggedly handsome as ever in his tan chamois shirt, jeans and boots. "No clue!" he said, stopping just short of her.

Ignoring the way her heart skittered in response whenever she was near him, Sara smiled proudly. "Charley got his first tooth!"

"You're kidding!"

She pointed to her son, who was enjoying some tummy time on his play mat in the middle of the living room floor. "See for yourself."

Matt sauntered over, laconic as ever, and stretched out beside Charley so the two were facing each other. Suddenly looking so very much like father and son it made her heart ache. If only Matt could be Charley's new daddy!

Oblivious to her wish, Matt gently cupped Charley's chin. "Going to let me see, big fella?"

Charley offered a huge grin.

Matt admired the edge of white peeking up out of his lower gum. "Wow."

Charley's grin widened all the more.

Matt peered closer, tilting his head. "Looks like the one next to it is about to push through, too."

Sara joined them on the blanket, kneeling beside them.

Beaming, she predicted, "Before we know it, he'll have two teeth!"

Charley gurgled and pounded the floor beneath him with his tiny fists. Rocking forward and back as if that alone would get him somewhere.

"Now, if we could just teach him to crawl instead of roll to where he wants to go," Sara sighed.

Charlie flipped over onto his side, again and again, until he found the toy he wanted and put it in his mouth.

"He'll get there," Matt reassured her, confident as ever. The corners of his eyes crinkled. "In the meantime, we should definitely celebrate his first tooth."

"We should," Sara agreed.

Merriment tugged at Matt's smile. "Think he's too young for ice cream?"

Doing something that fun, even with their tiny chaperones along, always seemed like a dangerous proposition to her way too vulnerable heart. She cleared her throat and lifted her chin. "I imagine he could have a little." It was time they expanded their repertoire of social expeditions again. That did not have to mean they'd end up holding hands or kissing or being tempted to make love again.

Especially if they kept things absolutely casual and platonic.

"You think?" Matt's eyes glittered with anticipation.

Sara nodded, reassuring herself they were doing the right thing. She smiled over at him. "It's such a nice day. The Dairy Barn in town would be a good place to socialize Champ, too."

His gaze traveled over the hollow of her throat, past her lips, to her eyes. He rose and offered her a hand up. "Let's go, then."

Half an hour later, they were pulling into the lot.

As always during their excursions, Matt took charge of Charley, while Sara snapped a leash on Champ and lifted him out of the car.

No sooner had they stepped onto the sidewalk, than a trio of delighted squeals rose from the other side of the decorative fence surrounding the outdoor eating area.

Matt lifted a hand in recognition. "Hey, Jack!" he called to his brother, as Jack's three little girls came running for them, all talking at once.

"It's the puppy, Champ! He's so cute! Can we pet him?"

"Sure." Sara stopped.

"Fancy seeing you two here," Jack said.

Matt shrugged. "We're friends."

A lift of the brow. "Friends? Lulu said you went on a date."

Matt remained impassive. "We did."

"And?" Jack pressed.

Another shrug. "Went right back into the friends zone."

The surgeon clapped a hand on Matt's shoulder, and spared Sara a genial look. "Mind if I have a word with my little brother?"

"Go right ahead."

Matt walked off, Charley still in his arms, Jack at his side. The three little girls gathered around Champ. Cooing over him and petting him by turn.

"Are you nuts?" Sara heard Jack say. "She's everything you'd ever want in a woman. And she's got a baby you clearly adore."

Mortified, Sara stood frozen in place.

Matt held his brother's assessing gaze with one of his own. "Just helping out."

Was that all it was? Sara wondered, stung by Matt's "this means nothing to me, so stop asking" tone.

The two men continued staring each other down. "Looks like a hell of a lot more than that to me," Jack harrumphed.

Matt scowled, looking trapped.

The three girls went from sitting to standing. Champ continued basking in the adoration.

"Yeah, well, maybe you don't know everything, Jack."

Jack leaned in, his own grief evident. "I know one thing. A woman who hits every wish on your list doesn't come along every day. And when you find her, you have to hold on. 'Cause if you don't...' Jack's voice cracked.

Too late, Sara realized it was coming up on the anniversary of his wife's death. Matt must have realized it, too.

"You're right," Matt said quietly, lifting a palm. "I'm an ass."

"No. I'm sorry." Jack scrubbed a hand over his face. "I shouldn't be pushing you. I just hate to see anyone else give up what they could have, while they still have a chance."

Aware she'd been eavesdropping for far too long, Sara stepped back, looked down. Swiftly became aware the little girls that had been surrounding her were gone... and that she was holding an empty leash.

She gasped.

Then turned in the direction of another trio of excited squeals.

There was Champ, nosing happily along the cement, with the girls accompanying him. And he was almost to the sidewalk that fronted the parking lot! Cars were turning in...backing out.

"Stop!" Sara shouted, fisting the leash and breaking into a run.

Spying what was going on, Jack hopped the waist-high fence.

Her heart pounding, Sara caught up with the puppy and Jack's youngest child. Her arms spread wide, she scooped both of them into the safety of her arms, then for good measure snapped the leash on Champ. Jack lassoed his two older daughters. Matt was suddenly there, too, Charley still cradled safely against his broad chest.

To Sara's immense relief, everyone was all right.

"You girls know better," Jack scolded.

The hell of it was, so did Sara.

Chapter Twelve

"You can take a breath now," Matt said to Sara, several hours later. They'd brought home takeout for dinner, and he'd stayed to help her for a while after that. Charley was upstairs, in bed, fast asleep for the night, and an exhausted Champ was curled up in the back of his crate, snoozing, too.

"Maybe even try to relax?" He flashed her a sexy half smile, even as worry darkened his eyes.

Sara only wished she could but try as she might she could not seem to let go of the near accident.

She lifted the ice pop mold out of the dishwasher. "I keep seeing it, over and over in my mind," she confessed. She carefully poured diluted fruit juice into each cup of the mold, then slid a pacifier-style holder into each slot.

She slanted a glance over her shoulder at Matt, then headed for the fridge. He opened the door to the freezer compartment for her.

"It all happened so fast," she lamented softly, setting the tray on a shelf.

She shut the door and turned back to Matt.

Unbidden, an image of Champ headed merrily for the parking lot, Jack's three little girls tagging innocently along beside him, flashed in her mind. And her heart once again filled with terror.

What if she hadn't happened to become aware at that precise instant?

Not looked up and seen...

A huge tragedy could have ensued.

And it would have been all her fault for being momentarily inattentive.

Without warning, her eyes filled and her throat ached. "Oh, Matt," she whispered shakily, putting her hands over her face, as the overwhelming guilt she'd been holding back all afternoon came rushing to the fore.

He moved closer, his understanding, intuitive nature and strong male presence like a port in the storm. He wrapped his arms around her. Moving one hand over her spine, threading the other through her hair, the action as comforting as his presence.

And yet the horrifying images inside her head, the emotion building inside her, did not subside. She gulped around her tears, shaking her head, aware she felt nearly as grief-stricken and guilty now as she had when she'd sent Anthony out on that completely unnecessary errand, only to have him die... "A split second later and..."

He held her closer still, bending down to press his cheek against the top of her head. "But it didn't happen, darlin'," he pointed out gruffly, wrapping his arms tighter around her.

Sara shuddered, tears still sliding down her face, even as she soaked up his warmth and his strength.

Was this how distressed he'd felt when Mutt was killed? And if so, how had he gotten over it?

All she knew for certain was that in the midst of the calamity he'd stayed really chill, and he was just as calm now. Laudably so. Despite his worry over her.

And while the intellectual part of her admired his unflappable attitude and his ability to simply take the near-catastrophe in stride, her intuitive side worried he might be shutting down emotionally again, the way he had been when they'd first started hanging out.

And that would not be good.

Not at all.

Matt frowned as his cell phone dinged.

Reluctantly, he let go of her and pulled the phone from his pocket. Seeing who it was from, he relaxed and moved to show her, too.

On screen, there was a text message with photo from Jack. Matt clicked over to the attached photo, smiling fondly. "Looks like the girls sent you an apology drawing."

Sara moved in close to see, her shoulder nudging the solid, warm musculature of Matt's chest. The artwork slash note was really cute. With a lot of grass, a puppy on a leash and a stick figure with Sara's name underneath. There were also hearts and flowers, and a big "We R So Soree!" printed across the top.

The message from Jack said, Sara: Chloe understands that although she likes to unhook things a lot, she cannot ever unsnap a puppy's leash from its collar again. (In case you can't figure out the spelling, they are so sorry, and so am I.) Thanks again for helping to save the day. Have a great evening.

Sara sighed. "Well, at least your big brother seems to have forgiven my inattention," she said.

"Now," Matt countered, with a wry smile, "all you have to do is forgive yourself."

Easier said than done, Sara thought.

Although, both men were right. She couldn't keep dwelling on past mistakes. Any more than she could dwell on Anthony's death. All she could do was behave a lot more responsibly in the future.

She went back to the rest of her evening chores: washing Charley's teething rings, putting them back in the freezer to chill, along with the homemade iced fruit pops, and emptying the dishwasher. As she did so, she spied the cartons, too. "You know we never did have that ice cream," she said, bringing out the two striped cartons.

Matt's eyes glinted. "I think I could handle that."

"Butter pecan or coconut almond?"

Matt set his phone aside and lounged against the counter, settling in comfortably and keeping her company, the way he had before they'd decided to put on the brakes. With a warm smile, he teased, "How about a little of both?"

"Sounds good." Sara scooped ice cream into two bowls.

It felt so right, having him with her. She knew she could get used to it. Was that what Matt's family was seeing, too? she wondered, as they sat down at the island, side by side, and began to eat. Why they were matchmaking and pushing her in his direction and vice versa?

Maybe this was something she and Matt did need to frankly discuss if they wanted to avoid awkward encounters in the future. She took a deep breath and turned to face him once again, her bent knees nearly brushing his. "Listen," she said, her spoon idling halfway to her lips, "about what Jack said to you about me…"

Still savoring the bite in his mouth, he grinned. "You *were* eavesdropping, then."

She heaved a sigh of relief at the realization he was amused instead of annoyed by her interest. "Yes," she said, trying not to blush. "I am deeply ashamed to admit that I was."

His brow furrowed. "Just out of curiosity…why were you so interested in what Jack was saying?"

Ignoring the butterflies in her stomach, Sara shrugged. Not about to admit how important it was to her, to be accepted as a suitable friend or companion by Matt's family.

"Because I had initially heard enough to know Jack was talking about me and you."

Needing to know more about what Matt was thinking and feeling, too, she forced herself to go on. "I also knew he was jumping to some pretty outrageous conclusions." Like in some way she and Matt were meant to be, the way Jack and Gayle had been.

An intimate silence fell.

"Yeah, well…" Matt shrugged, not the least bit surprised by his older brother's outburst. "He's still pretty angry about losing his wife in childbirth." Matt's voice dropped a sympathetic notch. "Having to raise Chloe from day one without her mom. And deal with Nicole and Lindsay's grief."

Sara reflected on the unbearable tragedy. "I can't even imagine how hard that has been for him."

With a commiserating nod, Matt finished the rest of

his dessert and put his dish aside. Understanding lit his gray-blue eyes. "Sometimes he's okay. He just sort of soldiers on and keeps everything in perspective." Matt exhaled. "At other times, like this afternoon, when he thinks that someone is *not* appreciating what they have, while they have it…" Matt's lips thinned "…he loses it and lets them have it."

Sara understood that kind of irrational jealousy and resentment. She'd suffered flashes of it herself, when in the early throes of her grief over her husband's death.

Matt rubbed at the taut muscles on the back of his neck. "The only problem is, of course," he observed, in a low, matter-of-fact tone, "that not everyone has the kind of love Jack shared with Gayle."

Was Matt talking about himself now? Sara wondered. The fact he had never loved anyone the way Jack had loved his late wife?

Hard to tell.

What she could absolutely discern was that Matt was conflicted about his past, his present and his future, just as she was.

Maybe because whether he wanted to admit it or not, the near miss of an accident with his nieces—and Champ—that day had inadvertently brought up his issues with Mutt, too. Although, no one on the scene at the Dairy Barn, aside from her and Matt, had known about that tragedy.

Deciding it would help them both to relax even further, she stood and beckoned him toward the adjacent living room.

Leaving him to follow at will, she said over her shoulder, "We've talked a lot about me. Not much about you." She sat down, patting the place beside her on the sofa.

As the silence stretched out, the tension between them increased.

"How are you doing?" she prodded.

He came only so far as the edge of the rug in the conversation area. Stood, legs braced slightly apart, thumbs hooked through the loops on either side of his fly.

"What do you mean?" he asked, as if it were no big deal.

Sara waited for him to join her on the sofa.

When he didn't, she pointed out, "You were pretty cheerful when we set out to celebrate Charley's first tooth today. Since Champ was inadvertently let loose…not as cheerful."

His gaze narrowed. "Maybe I just have a lot on my mind."

"Like what…?" she pressed.

"Like, you really *don't* have to rescue me."

The fact she was able to get under his skin so easily, meant he was feeling something. Determined to find out what, she murmured, "I know."

He gave her a deeply irritated look that said, *Do you?*

Feeling a little like she'd just grabbed a lion by the tail, she rose and crossed to his side. As she inhaled the musky scent of him, her heart did a funny little twist in her chest. "You can still lean on me, the way I've been leaning on you the past few weeks."

His expression didn't change in the slightest. Yet he exuded testosterone with every slow, even breath.

"I don't need to lean on you."

And isn't that just the problem. Sara sighed, lamenting the fact this was not the first time she'd found herself in this situation, although she desperately wanted it to be the last.

Heat bloomed in her cheeks. Achingly aware of just how much she was coming to care for him, not just as a friend, but as the most important man in her life, she said softly, "You could if you wanted."

He looked at her for a long moment. "And if I don't...?" he asked.

Sara tamped down the fantasies their previous love-making sessions had inspired.

She shrugged, not sure whether to be relieved he was keeping the brakes on the chemistry between them. Or hurt that he wasn't as interested in getting to intimately understand each other as she was.

"Then we don't really have a relationship that is at all equal."

He met her gaze, his eyes dark and heated. "And that's a problem because...?"

"Lopsided friendships never work," she explained, her voice every bit as exasperated as his had been. "At least not long term. And right now," she huffed, wishing she didn't want to kiss him again so very much, "*I* seem to be doing all the taking, while *you're* doing all the giving."

And that was unfair.

He put a hand around her waist and tugged her against him. Then he leaned over and whispered in her ear, "Maybe I like it that way."

The unyielding imprint of his tall, strong body had her nipples tingling and pressing against her shirt. "Yeah, well, cowboy, maybe I don't."

He met her gaze in a way that made all rational thinking cease.

She thought about making love with him.

Holding him through the night.

Waking up together.

And most important, getting closer emotionally.

She had the strong impression he knew what she was beginning to want. And yearned for it, too. But for reasons she couldn't understand, wasn't about to let either of them have it.

He cleared his throat. To her frustration, every barrier that had ever been around his heart, seemed to be firmly back in place. "I probably should be heading home."

Suddenly, that was the last thing Sara wanted. Sensing she wasn't the only one who needed more love and attention in her life, she moved closer still.

This was one of those watershed moments.

"What if I want you to stay, Matt?" she asked, daring to put her own feelings on the line, to admit she wanted to feel incredibly close to him again. The way they felt when they were making love. She paused to look him in the eye. Asked softly, "What, then?"

Matt let his gaze drift over her, taking in every sweet, supple inch. She was so beautiful, so bright and intuitive and incredibly feminine. Had she not been in such a vulnerable state...

But she was.

And, having been raised a gentleman, he could not take advantage of that.

"Probably not a good idea," he said gruffly. Especially when he wanted to make love to her again as much as he did.

The fire of indignation lit her jade eyes. She stepped back, all cordial Texas grace. "Why not?"

He searched for some inner nobility that would give her all she needed—and nothing to later regret. Ignoring the way-too-innocent sparkle in her eyes, he tightened his fingers over hers and leaned in close enough to inhale the fragrance of her skin and hair. Then he let his gaze move wistfully from the playful curve of her lips, back to her eyes. "Because I don't trust myself not to kiss you again," he said, unable to help but admire how pretty and sassy she looked, with her pink cheeks and tousled hair.

Reluctantly, he let her go, stepped back. "And since we agreed to stay in the 'just friends' zone from here on out…"

She reached up to remove the clip from her hair and set it aside. He watched the wavy golden-blond mass fall loose and free to her shoulders once again.

Her lusciously soft lower lip shot out. "What if that, too, was a mistake?"

With Herculean effort, he resisted the urge to pull her right back into his arms. "Look, Sara, I get that you had an incredibly upsetting experience today and you're still shaken up." Just as he was. "You probably still have a lot of adrenaline running through you. But now isn't the time to leap recklessly into something you will later regret."

Sara scowled, her frustration with the situation apparent. "Making love with you is not what I've been regretting, Matt." She looked him straight in the eye. "Pushing you away, trying to put our relationship into some preconceived, predetermined box with boundaries that don't even make any sense, is what I've been regretting."

She was making a powerful argument. And if she hadn't been so susceptible… He swallowed. "You deserve to be married again."

"And I've told *you* that I don't want that!"

Maybe not now. He was pretty sure that would change when she got over the loss of her late husband.

"Charley needs—"

Sara went up on tiptoe. Cut him off with a finger pressed against his lips. "Charley needs people around him who love him and care for him," she asserted in a low, determined tone. "He needs strong, male role models in his life." She encircled her arms about his neck, fitting her soft, supple body against the length of his. "You fill both those needs."

Feeling himself grow instantly hard, it was all Matt could do not to groan. Summoning up every bit of chivalry he had, he unhooked her arms and set her aside. "And I'd like to do so in the future."

She smiled, not the least bit dissuaded. "Great. Charley and I want the same." She reached down to take off her boots.

Mouth dry, he watched her begin to unbutton her blouse. "It's not that simple, Sara."

Passion gleamed in her pretty eyes. She stripped off her shirt. Reached for the zipper on her jeans. "Why isn't it?"

He caught her hand before she could shimmy out of her jeans. "Because once again you're not addressing what you need."

"Yes, Matt, I am." She moved into his arms, taking the initiative and pressing her lips to his. With a low growl, he found himself succumbing to the desire he had promised himself, for both their sakes, he would never resurrect again. Blood thundered through him, and he reveled in the taste and feel of her. Yet he knew what he had to do.

With a groan of frustration, he sifted his hands through her hair and tore his mouth away. "Sara…"

Her lower lip, so soft and pink and bare, trembled slightly. Yet her feisty resolve remained.

She splayed her hands across his chest. She kissed his jaw, the skin behind his ear. "I want you to stay, Matt." Her nipples protruded from the satin of her bra as she reached for the buttons on his shirt. Twin spots of color brightened her high cheekbones. "I want us to go back to making love, and being there for each other, whenever, however, we each need," she confessed softly, vulnerability shimmering in her pretty green eyes. "While at the same time," she continued persuasively, "not judging each other for any of our flaws. Or resenting each other for what we can't seem to give."

Hands on her shoulders, he forced himself not to think about taking her to bed again. "We need to slow down, darlin'," he warned. "Talk about this."

"Why?" Hurt warred with the frustration in her eyes. "When I feel like you get me and accept me the way no one else does, or ever will! I want to be close to you, Matt. Closer than we've been this last week." Her slender body trembled. "What is so wrong with that?"

Nothing. At least so far as he could figure in his heart. He could hardly chastise her for wanting to live her life to the fullest in any way she chose, when he was resolved to do the very same thing in his. "You make a compelling argument," he said gruffly.

"Good." She guided him over to the sofa. As soon as he sat down, she slid onto his lap. "Now, where were we?"

Saying to heck with caution, he reached around behind her and unhooked her bra. "In a wagonful of trouble."

She laughed softly. "Trouble can be fun…"

He cupped her breasts, his body hardening as he felt her quiver. "Pretty much everything about you is fun."

She lowered her face to his. "Right back at you, cowboy," she murmured back, then kissed him with a sensuality that further rocked his world. Her soft pliant form surrendering against his, she threaded her hands through his hair, moaning softly. He cupped the silky globes of her breasts with both hands, drawing first one rosy bud, then the other into his mouth. And still she melted against him and held him as if she never wanted to let him go.

Loving her unfettered response, he lifted his head. Exhilarated by the fact she was about to be his…again… he rasped, "Any special requests?"

She laughed softly. "Your choice."

Pure male satisfaction poured through him. "Even better."

He eased his palm past the edge of her panties, finding the damp, soft nest. She moaned as he stroked. Eager to please her, he kept kissing her, while continuing his slow, sensual exploration. He stroked her repeatedly, light butterfly touches that had her shuddering. Kisses and caresses that had her melting.

They switched places and he knelt before her, stripped off her panties and positioned himself between her thighs. Holding her open to him. Loving her. Until she twisted against him, no longer able to hide the totality of her response.

As eager to please him as he had been her, she unbuttoned his belt, undid his fly. Slipping her hands inside, she found the hot, hard length of him.

Their reactions were simultaneous. He groaned. She trembled with pleasure.

Caught up in something too elemental to fight, she

bent to love him. Until he, too, could stand it no more. He found a condom. Together, they rolled it on.

With a growl of satisfaction, he stretched out over top of her and brought his whole body into contact with hers. Hands beneath her hips, he spread her thighs and slid inside, penetrating deep. She gasped and kissed him back, to his delight, just as ravenous for him as he was for her. And then they slowed it down. Taking their time. Drawing out the unimaginable pleasure. Until there was no more holding back, no more waiting. She was wrapping her legs around his waist, drawing him deeper, surrendering to his will, even as powerful sensations layered, one over another.

He lay claim to her lips and her body, as he wanted to lay claim to her heart and soul. Until she was kissing him back, more ardently than ever before. And this time, when they came together in shattering pleasure, he knew there was no going back, for either of them.

For long moments they lay locked together, quivering with delicious aftershocks of their passion, catching their breath. Worried he might be too heavy for her, he rolled onto his side.

She moved with him. Emitting a happy sigh, said, "I have to tell you, cowboy, I could sooo get used to this."

He propped his head on his elbow and gazed deep into her eyes. "Same here, darlin'." He stroked his fingers through her tousled hair, pressed a gentle kiss on her temple.

Her gaze grew dreamy. "Want to spend the night?"

More than you'll ever know.

Wary that could ruin everything, however, he clasped her close and pressed another kiss on the top of her head. Wishing things were different, said, "Remember that speech you gave me earlier, about not asking or expecting us to give anything we don't feel able to?"

She nodded.

Rising, he reached for his clothes. "Well, this is one of those things I shouldn't do."

Hurt flickered briefly on her pretty face. "Because we're not married and not going to be?"

That is definitely part of it. But not all. Not nearly. "Because you'll sleep better without me here," he said.

Chapter Thirteen

To Sara's delight, the week that followed was a lot more romantically satisfying than the previous one. Matt showed up to help her every afternoon, then stayed for dinner and the bedtime routines for Charley and Champ. The only thing he wouldn't do…wouldn't even consider doing…was spend the night after they'd made love.

Which in turn made her ruminate. What was really preventing him from actually *sleeping* with her? Was he a bed hog? A restless sleeper? Insomniac? Did he snore? Just really hate to snuggle? Or did this have something to do with the PTSD she'd been suspecting he had? Sara couldn't begin to figure it out, and he didn't want to discuss it, so she was still wondering about his motivation when he arrived at her home late Friday afternoon, just in time for Champ's training session.

"What is he going to work on today?" Matt asked, cuddling Charley, who had just woken up from his nap.

"You'll see." Sara grinned, proud of how much progress the little black Lab was making.

Using a simultaneous combination of hand signal and verbal command, she walked Champ out to the back patio. Said, "Champ, sit!"

He put his rump on the ground, and kept his eyes on her.

"Stay!"

The pup remained perfectly still. She waited a second, then backed up several paces. "Champ, come!"

He rose and trotted to her side.

"Sit!"

He sat obediently.

She patted the ground in front of his paws. "Down."

Champ stretched out, his tummy on the ground, too.

"Good boy, Champ!" Still praising him warmly, Sara hunkered down beside him and petted the top of his head. "Good boy!"

She rose to her feet once again.

"Champ, stand."

He rose with canine grace. Stood looking patiently at her.

"Wow," Matt said. "He's got it all down pat."

Sara smiled proudly. "He does, doesn't he?" She took Champ's leash and led him over to his spot in the grass, where he promptly relieved himself. "I can't wait to show him off at the reunion picnic tomorrow."

"Any final word on where it's going to be yet?" he asked.

Sara nodded, not so happy about the predicted weather, and the necessary change in accommodations. "The rain is supposed to start around nine this evening and continue until midnight tomorrow. So the event has been moved to the WTWA building in Laramie."

Matt grinned down at Charley, who was now patting Matt's jaw with both of his little hands. He paused to kiss Charley's fingertips, then turned his attention back to Sara. "Will it hold everyone?"

She paused to let Champ get a drink from his outdoor water bowl, then led him back inside. "There are three levels of meeting rooms and a large covered patio out back, so yes, it will." Sara directed Champ to his mat on the floor and handed him a nylon chew bone.

She washed her hands, then took Charley from Matt and settled her son in the high chair next to her. "Although it won't be as accessible an event as usual, due to the fact everyone won't be scattered across one large space."

Looking devastatingly handsome in a blue chambray shirt and jeans, Matt lounged against the counter, arms folded in front of him. His hair was clean and rumpled and he smelled like soap and cologne. The faint hint of evening beard clung to his jaw.

"That's too bad," he said.

As intensely aware of him as ever, Sara shrugged. "It will still be fun." She walked into the pantry and emerged with canisters of flour, regular and confectioner's sugar, and a tin of cocoa.

He didn't look convinced but deftly dropped the subject.

"So. What are you making?" he asked, nodding at the eggs and butter coming to room temperature on the counter.

"Our contribution to the feast. Two large sheet pans of fudge brownies."

He waggled his brows in anticipation. "Can I help?"

She handed him the box of Cheerios for Charley. "Keep me company. And lend a hand if either of our two little ones need something."

Matt scattered dry cereal on Charley's tray. "They look pretty content right now," he observed.

Charley was snacking on Cheerios, watching everything that was going on around him, while Champ was lying on the floor next to Sara, his nylon puppy chew bone clasped between his little paws.

"They do."

Sara slipped a chef's apron over her neck.

Matt stepped behind her to tie it, his hands brushing her spine in the process.

Tingling from even the light contact, Sara smiled her thanks and stepped back to the counter to consult the recipe. "Hard to believe it's his last night here."

Matt watched as she broke eight eggs into a bowl.

"You going to be okay, saying goodbye to Champ tomorrow?" he asked in the gruff-tender voice she loved.

Aware it was her turn to keep her feelings tightly locked away, Sara put the softened butter and sugar into the bowl, and turned the stand mixer on low. "I probably wouldn't be if I hadn't made a point to not get too attached to him." She forced herself to focus on the task at hand. "But I know he's going to be with Alyssa Barnes and her family." And that was, she knew, a very good thing for the returning wounded soldier and Champ.

Matt nodded his approval. "They were really nice when we met them."

Sara measured vanilla into the wet ingredients. "And she's so excited about working with him, which will in turn help her in own recovery."

Matt stepped back to give her room when she added the flour and cocoa to the mixing bowl. He looked down at Champ, and Sara thought, but couldn't be sure, Matt had a brief gleam of affection in his eyes.

He looked back at Sara, his expression implacable again. "How long will Alyssa Barnes have him?"

"About two years, or however long it takes for him to complete all of his training and be permanently paired with a disabled veteran." Sara spooned the batter into the pans. "At which point, she'll have a chance to start all over again, with another puppy." Finished, she removed the paddle and offered it to him. "Which is what most of the program volunteers do. Helping out like that can be pretty gratifying."

He scooped off a taste with his fingertip and then gave it back to her. "I can see that."

She savored the chocolate mixture, too. And thought about kissing him again. Knowing that if she did, he would not only taste like rich chocolate brownie batter, but also the dark male essence unique to him.

Aware she was running out of time with Champ and Matt, she gathered her courage and said, "By the way, I know our deal was for one month." Which had flown by way too fast. "But I want you to know," she said huskily, "you are welcome here anytime."

Matt wrapped his arms around her waist and brought her close for one long, sweet kiss. Melting into the embrace, she kissed him back, sliding her hands across his solid muscular chest. When he'd finished, he looked down at her tenderly. "You and Charley are welcome at my ranch, too. Anytime." He rubbed his thumb across her lower lip, clearly savoring their time together every bit as much as she. "No invitation required."

* * *

Sara and Matt spent the rest of the evening, sharing a quick and easy dinner, and caring for Charley and Champ. When both little ones were down for the night, he helped her cut up the cooled brownies and pack them into foil serving pans.

"Tomorrow's going to be a long day," he said, when they'd finished. "I probably better head on home."

Maybe it was presumptuous of her, but she'd been looking forward to whiling away the rest of the evening with him, now that their little ones were fast asleep.

"Sure?" she said. "There's a new movie on Netflix you might enjoy." She grinned saucily. "I've got popcorn..."

He shook his head. "Thanks, but...some other time, okay?"

He brought her close for a scorching hot good-night kiss, hugged her one last time, then smiled again and slipped out the door.

Flummoxed, Sara stood on the porch waving as he drove away. It wasn't the first time he had exited before ten in the evening, or even the first time he had left without making love with her during the last week.

Since their "misunderstanding," he had been working hard to refrain from any behavior that might seem at all overfamiliar.

To treat her with courtesy and respect and make sure she knew that as much as he appreciated and desired her, that he also respected her space, and her need for privacy.

But tonight his courteous exit felt different somehow. Like some mysterious wall was between them. Like there was something he didn't want her to see.

And late the next morning when he arrived to take her

and Charley and Champ into town, he was even more scrupulously polite.

"Is this everything?" he asked, as he stacked Champ's food and water bowls, chew toys, sleep towel and leash in a box on top of his travel and sleeping crate.

"Just about." Sara looked at the water sluicing off the eaves. She slipped on her raincoat and hat. "I just need to take him out to go one last time before we head out."

The only problem was, Champ didn't like the rain or the wet ground. She walked him around and around on his leash, waiting for him to squat and relieve himself. To no avail.

He was having none of it.

Finally, Sara gathered him in her arms and took him inside the house. He was soaked to the skin and shivering. She was equally drenched.

Matt handed her a towel from the stack by the back door. Sara started with Champ's head and ears, and gently blotted the moisture from his silky black fur. As much as she could, anyway. Then she worked her way over his shoulders, down beneath his belly and legs, and paws. He leaned into her, snuggling close, the way he had so many times, and suddenly it hit her. This was the very last time he would be her responsibility. The tears she'd been holding back flooded her eyes.

She blinked them away furiously. Matt turned away. But not before she saw the moisture shimmering in his eyes, too.

Was this what he'd been hiding from her the previous evening? The fact that despite all common sense, he'd gotten attached to little Champ, too?

Several hours later, Garrett Lockhart, the doctor and former army captain who helmed the WTWA and also ran his family's charitable foundation, caught up with Matt near the buffet tables. The one place in the facility where, to Matt's relief, dogs weren't allowed.

"Hey." Garrett grinned at Matt who was there hanging out with Charley. "I just met Champ. You and Sara did a great job bringing the little pup along. He's incredibly relaxed and outgoing."

Except, Matt thought guiltily as Charley kicked his foot against his chest, dislodging his baby moccasin in the process, *he* hadn't done much of anything to help socialize Champ. Yes, he had cared for baby Charley while Sara worked with the cute little puppy. And he'd supervised Champ for a couple of hours while Sara grabbed some much needed sleep. He'd also helped Champ acclimate to his training crate. But he hadn't stopped to personally greet or pet him, or cuddle him the way Sara did, even once.

Not about to publicly admit that, though, Matt smiled, demonstrating the cheerful attitude the event attendees expected to see from him.

"All Sara's doing," he admitted with a shrug, while trying to retie Charley's shoe with one hand. Not easy, given the way Charley was situated in the BabyBjörn hooked over Matt's shoulders. "All I did was watch over Charley here while Sara did all the work."

"Speaking of baby wrangling…" Hope, Garrett's wife, interjected. She smiled when Charley kicked his moccasin all the way off and it went sailing in the air between them. Then bent to pick it up and moved forward to help put it back on. "I have to ask. How *did* Sara talk you into doing that?"

Matt chuckled. This was a little easier to talk about. "Let's just say she's persistent," he teased.

Garrett wrapped his arm around his wife's shoulder, as their five-year-old son, Max, and his little brother, Harry, played peekaboo around their parents' legs. "The mark of a good woman." He bussed his wife's head. "She never gives up."

Hope leaned her head on Garrett's shoulder. "Not when it comes to love, anyway."

The problem was, Sara wasn't in love with him, Matt thought. The only thing she saw him as was a good friend and part-time lover, and although both of them had started out wanting nothing more than that, he was beginning to think they'd been wrong to limit themselves. If they ever wanted to have what Hope and Garrett Lockhart and some of his happily married siblings had, anyway.

And speaking of brothers...

Bess Monroe, Jack and his three little girls came up to join them. "Where's Sara?" they asked in unison.

Matt inclined his head. "Upstairs in one of the meeting rooms on the second floor, convening with all the rest of the dogs in Champ's litter."

Matt looked at Jack and Bess. Was it his imagination or did the two of them have something going on? Besides the decades-long friendship they claimed? His brother had interfered in his love life. Maybe it was time he did the same. "What are you-all doing here together?"

Bess smiled, as Charley's shoe once again went sailing. She knelt to pick it up and handed it to Matt, then nodded at Jack and his daughters. "They're my plus four," she bragged. "Saved me from needing an actual date."

"And—" Jack looked at his daughters fondly "—they wanted to see Champ and make sure he was still all right, after that unfortunate incident at the Dairy Barn."

Matt pointed them in the right direction. And then pretended to need to find a quiet place, to change Charley's diaper and feed him his bottle.

And so it went for the rest of the day.

Charley kept kicking off the one shoe and stayed mostly with Matt, while Sara went back and forth, talking to everyone she'd been working with in the puppy raising program for the last two years, and helping out with the replenishment of the buffet.

Matt stayed on the sidelines as much as possible, glad he had Charley to both distract and run interference for him.

"You didn't get to do as much socializing as I did," Sara lamented much later, when they drove home.

Relieved the event was over, Matt exhaled. "Actually, Charley attracted plenty of people. All of whom wanted to tell me just how cute he was."

Sara grinned with maternal pride. "He is that."

The advantage of carrying around a baby had also prevented him from paying direct attention to any of the service dogs. It had still been hard being at the reunion, though, Matt reflected tensely. Because everywhere he had gone, there had been an active or retired military person and a service dog, reminding him once again of what he really didn't want to remember.

"Hard to believe Charley is still wide-awake at nine o'clock at night," Matt said.

"Probably has something to do with all that time he spent sleeping on your chest today, at the reunion," Sara mused, bringing in two mugs of coffee for the adults. Hers had cream, no sugar. Matt's was plain, just the way he liked it. Which was no surprise. She did everything just the way he liked it.

She settled next to him on the floor, turning toward him in a drift of lilac perfume. Pretty color highlighted the delicate planes of her cheeks. "You could have put him down, you know, let him sleep in his stroller."

"I know." It had been comforting, having Charley cuddled up against him. While at the same time experiencing what it would feel like if Charley were actually his son.

She looked at him over the rim of her mug, enthusiasm still glittering in her eyes. "What did you think about the event?"

That it had gone on way, way too long. For him, anyway. For everyone else it had concluded far too soon.

He took a sip of his coffee, and found it as perfectly brewed as always. "It's a good organization."

Her soft, bare lips formed a sexy smile. "Thinking of joining it?"

Given the way he was feeling right now? No. He also knew what Sara hoped to hear. And for reasons he couldn't begin to decipher, he did not want to disappoint her. "Maybe later," he hedged. That was, if his plan to keep desensitizing himself to dogs worked as he hoped.

Determined to steer the conversation away from the stuff that still haunted him, he returned his full attention to Charley, who was still stretched out on the play rug between them. Head up, his tummy flat on the floor, he was trying to pull himself forward by moving his arms. Unfortunately, he did not have the strength for his weight.

Matt smiled tenderly. He shifted the toy Charley had his eye on a little closer. Charley reacted by bouncing up and down, the movement just enough to allow him to capture the stuffed ducky.

He chuckled. "Got to hand it to the little fella. He's still trying to figure things out."

Sara sighed with maternal frustration.

Matt knew she wanted to solve all her son's problems for him. Rather than let him work this out for himself.

"I've been trying to show him how to crawl," Sara said.

"Oh yeah?" Matt waggled his brows, attempting to tease her into relaxing about her son's lack of progress on the physical agility front. He nudged her bent knee playfully with his. "Want to try teaching me?"

She returned his look with mock indignation. "No."

He chuckled, playing along with her stern reproach.

Sara watched her son roll right back over on his tummy and begin the search for a way to crawl again.

She took a deep breath, continued bringing him up to date. "I've stretched out right beside him and got up on all fours, and rocked back and forth, just as he is now, and then demonstrated it to him by moving one arm and leg forward slowly, and then the other."

Interesting.

And something he really would not have thought of doing himself.

But then, he'd been brought up to be a McCabe man and McCabe men solved their own problems.

"And what does he do?" Matt asked.

Listening to the adult conversation, Charley lifted his belly up off the floor, and began rocking back and forth in earnest.

Sara ran her hands through the silky strands of her hair. "Usually he just plops down and looks at me as if to say, *What in the world are you doing, Mom?* And then he rolls around to get whatever he wants."

Matt shrugged. "Well, as long as he's mobile."

Sara's lower lip shot out in frustration. "It's important he achieves this milestone."

"Even if he's not quite ready?" Matt said, as Charley planted both hands and feet on the floor, and then lifted his tummy and bottom as high as he possibly could, a move that put his body into an inverted U. As usual, he got stuck in that position, and let out a frustrated scream.

Sara reached over to help her son get unstuck and fall gently back into a seated position. "I honestly think he'd be happier if he could get around." She handed Charley a small stuffed blue bunny.

He lifted it to his mouth, and chewed on a corner earnestly.

Matt looked around. With all the dog paraphernalia gone, the living area seemed oddly barren. He soothed Sara as best he could. "Well, it won't be as hard for you to work on this with Charley, now that Champ isn't here."

Sara immediately teared up. She looked like she had lost her best friend.

"Sorry," Matt said hastily.

Shaking her head in abject misery, she rose, ducked into the nearby powder room and shut the door behind her.

Matt looked at Charley. Glad he was too young to understand that Sara was crying. He leaned forward conspiratorially. "I know your mommy *says* it's too much but we may have to get her a puppy of her very own— to keep."

Sara came back out of the bathroom, her spine stiff with indignation. She glared at Matt. "Don't you dare."

He was about to ask why not, when she lifted a silencing palm.

"I have to get over the loss first," she explained firmly. "And then, and only then, will I consider what else might be in our future."

Sara used the time upstairs, getting Charley ready for bed and tucked in, to further compose herself. When she came back down, to her surprise, Matt had put their coffee mugs in the dishwasher. His hat, rain jacket and cell phone were nearby.

"You're getting ready to leave?" she asked in surprise, aware she had been acting a little hormonal.

Or maybe just grief-stricken.

She really had gotten used to having the little puppy around. Even though she had known all along she would not be able to keep him.

He shrugged, his emotions as tightly wrapped up as hers had been vividly on display. "I figured it's been a really long day."

She caught his arm before he could move past her, her fingers closing over the swell of his bicep. She knew she'd been crabby. She also knew he'd been sort of withdrawn and brooding all day.

She'd thought maybe it was because there were so many dogs and military people at the reunion picnic. That it had been hard for him to be around that. Now she wondered if more was bothering him.

"I still have energy," she said. When it looked like he was going to protest, she lifted her palm in the age-old sign of peace. "You look like you do, too." She paused to look him in the eye, figuring if she couldn't help her son learn to crawl, she could at least encourage Matt to open up to her about what was bothering him. "So what's really going on here, Matt?"

He held her eyes with his mesmerizing gaze, making her feel all hot and bothered. "You want me to be blunt?"

She checked her need to throw herself into his arms and kiss him until all her excess emotions fled. His body language and curt tone made it clear he was not in the mood for romance.

"Of course."

He stuck his thumbs through the loops on either side of his fly and rocked back on his heels. "The reason I've been here almost every day the last month is now residing elsewhere with Alyssa Barnes."

She studied him in consternation. "Meaning what? I'd have to get another puppy for me to take care of in order to keep you dropping by on a regular basis?"

Frustration tautened the handsome planes of his face. Abruptly, he looked like he didn't know what to make of the new phase of their relationship, either.

With a sigh, he resumed his usual easygoing manner. "I love Charley. You know that." His gaze gentled. "I love hanging out with you, too."

"Love hanging out with" was not the same as *love*. At least not the kind she wanted, deep down. But maybe he was right. Maybe, like Charley's crawling, their relationship would continue to develop in its own way, its own time. *If* she didn't push. She jerked in a bolstering breath. "Then why not just build on that?" she asked softly.

A contemplative silence fell. Leaving her feeling like there was still so much she didn't know about him. Might never know, if it were up to him.

His gaze drifted over her, lingering on her lips before returning to her eyes. "You want to keep seeing each other as much as we have been?"

Sara nodded. "I want to keep making love with you, too."

He groaned, then, looking more conflicted than ever, said, "Sara... I know we said we'd just keep things casual and figure out what to do one day at a time...without making demands on each other. But maybe, given how upset you are at having to give up Champ, even though you knew all along this was coming..."

His words sounded perilously like a breakup speech.

Distraught to find herself close to losing even more in the space of one day, and all because he couldn't handle the loss they'd both been braced for any more than she could, she said, "I know you tried to keep your distance from Champ, and in a way, you did, but your heart aches, too, Matt. Don't deny it."

He scrubbed a hand over his face, abruptly looking as miserable and distraught as she felt. "Not trying to," he said gruffly.

She held out her hands imploringly. "Then what are you trying to do?" she asked, tears blurring her vision.

His expression immediately contrite, he moved farther away from her. "What I've been trying to do for weeks now. Look out for you and your needs," he said, his voice turning even raspier.

She knew he thought disappearing to deal with his grief would somehow spare her, the way he'd tried to spare his family after the attack on the compound. But it wouldn't. Not now, when the only two people in the world who knew exactly what they were feeling was themselves.

She studied him, her heart racing. "You want to be gallant? You want to care for me?"

Frustration warred with the exasperation on his face. "You know I do."

In a panic, fearing she would lose him, too, Sara

moved in and wrapped her arms around his neck. "Then kiss me, Matt," she whispered, lifting her lips to his. "Just kiss me."

And so he did.

Matt had never imagined he would be in a position to use the chemistry he had with Sara to gain entry to her heart. But their situation was so complicated he had no choice but to use whatever advantage he had to get close to her. To let her know he wanted her in his life, not as some occasional lover and casual friend, but as a real viable part of his everyday existence.

He wanted her to be able to come to him, as easily as he had been coming to see her the past month. He wanted to share her worries and her triumphs regarding Charley. Be there every evening for dinner, and be able to go home after to his place and know she not only understood, but was okay with it.

So when she took his hand and led him upstairs to her bed, he went. Kissing her the entire way.

And when she started to disrobe, he helped her. Just as she helped him.

Naked, he pulled her to the edge of the bed, knelt on the floor in front of her and nudged her thighs apart. She gasped and caught his head as he found her. Satisfaction roaring through him, he breathed in her sweet, musky scent and explored the silky heat, the taut pearly bud.

And still he ravished her, again and again, until she was calling his name and coming apart in his hands. Loving the no-holds-barred way she surrendered herself to him, he moved up again. Kissed her fiercely, deeply. Taking her the way she demanded to be taken, completely, irrevocably. Until there was no doubt she knew how much he wanted her. There was no stopping the building sensation. And she was clamped around him, urging him on to a soul-shattering climax, and then slowly, sweetly back down again.

For long moments after, they clung to each other. He savored the feel of her wrapped up in this arms, cognizant of just how fragile the moment was. Because he knew he was going to have to get up, get dressed and go home, if he didn't want to fall asleep.

And he would leave.

Eventually.

Once they'd both had their fill.

Right now, he needed and wanted to hold her, just a while longer.

Chapter Fourteen

Sara woke to the sound of a loud gasp and guttural moan, followed by a piercing "No" and the most primal scream of terror and agony she'd ever heard. She bolted upright at the same time as Matt, who was wild-eyed and sweating, swung both arms up to shield his face and reeled backward.

Swearing, he lunged forward, at least so far as the covers tangled around them would allow. Then let out another chilling shout of anguish. "Mutt! Oh my God!" His voice broke as tears streamed down his face. "Mutt!"

Before she knew it, Sara was crying, too.

Desperate to end his nightmare, she grabbed Matt's arms, attempting to wake him. At the same time, Charley started to cry in the nursery down the hall.

"Matt!" She shook his shoulders, harder now.

Still in the midst of his night terror, he threw her off.

Torn between her need to minister to Matt and comfort her son, Sara bolted from the bed. She grabbed her robe and raced down the hall, shrugging it on as she moved, listening to the heartbreaking sounds of her son's sobs, and the diminishing cries of Matt.

Her heart pounding, she switched on the nursery light and moved to her distraught son's side. "It's all right, baby, I'm here," she soothed, as she picked up her wailing infant and held him to her. She swept her hand reassuringly down his back. "Hush now, baby, Mommy's here. It was just a bad dream."

Charley burrowed his wet face into her shoulder. She sat down with him in the glider, and still crooning gently, began to rock back and forth .

Charley drew a shaky breath and snuggled even nearer, not crying now, but clinging to her as if his life depended on it.

She sang his favorite lullaby, felt him relax even more, as Matt's chaotic voice faded and the upstairs fell completely silent once again.

Eventually, Sara realized Charley was once again sound asleep.

Carefully, she eased him back into his crib. Stood there a moment, her hand resting lightly on his chest. She felt his breathing, deep and even. Relieved his own upset had been so short-lived, she turned and crept out of the nursery, walked down the hall into the master suite.

The king-size bed was empty.

Matt was dressing quietly in the moonlight. Head bowed, broad shoulders hunched forward in defeat, he looked as completely destroyed inside as she suddenly felt.

Not sure how to comfort him, she walked in. Her emotions in turmoil, she took a stabilizing breath. "You're awake."

He offered a terse nod in response, then boots in hand, headed past her without a word down the stairs.

Barely able to contain her hurt and confusion, Sara followed. She'd expected him to accept her comfort as readily as Charley had. Instead, he seemed to wish they were a thousand miles apart.

She understood he was embarrassed.

He had no reason to be.

Determined to make him understand and accept that, she intercepted him at the door. "You don't have to leave, Matt," she told him quietly. "In fact, I'd prefer you didn't. Not until we've at least had a chance to talk."

He shoved a hand through his hair and let out a long breath. Looking frustrated that she needed him to spell it out for her. Even though that was apparently the last thing he wanted to do.

More determined than ever not to part like this again, with both of them locked in their own private version of hell, she moved into the doorway, further blocking his exit. Ignoring the tight lines around his mouth and the shadows in his eyes, she asked, "Is this why you've never wanted to stay the night with me? Have you been having nightmares all along?"

Matt wasn't sure how to answer that, because first, he didn't want her to know how long and how often this had been going on. He didn't want anyone to know. And second, he wasn't exactly sure what had happened tonight.

Only that their lovemaking had been more incredible than ever. He hadn't intended to fall asleep and tempt fate. But she'd wanted him to stay a little longer and he'd been too damn weak and greedy to say no. So he'd cuddled her close, savoring the delicious feel of her soft body pressed up against his. The next thing he knew, he was waking up, sweating and alone, to the sounds of Sara running down the hall, baby Charley crying his heart out. The state of the bedcovers, his own pounding pulse, echoing shouts and aching throat had him surmising the rest...

He'd been dreaming about the compound again.

The suicide bombers.

The explosions...

And the sheer hell and heartbreak that had followed.

"Was your bad dream about Mutt?" she persisted, her soft hand curling around the taut muscles of his bicep.

Why deny it? Suddenly too weary to stand, he sat down on the stairs to pull on his boots. He had to get out of here, if he wanted even a prayer of shaking off the residual terror and grief. He also knew, after what she'd just witnessed, she wasn't going to let it go. So it was either talk it out now, or face it later.

"Have you been having nightmares?" she asked again, sitting next to him on the tread.

He grimaced. "Sometimes." But they had faded when he had started spending time with her and Charley and Champ. Not gone away entirely. But lessened, just the same.

Until tonight, anyway.

Tonight it had been as bad as it had ever been.

He blew out a breath.

She wound her hand through his. "Why didn't you tell me?"

He looked down at their entwined fingers, wishing they could forget all this and just go back to making love. "I did."

She studied him a long, heartrending moment. Compressed her soft lips together, but still left her hand in his. "Ah no, cowboy, you did not..."

Okay, so I didn't exactly confess to chronic night terrors. Tightly, he reminded her, "When I said you'd sleep better without me here...that I wasn't marriage material...that's what I meant."

She swiveled to face him, her bent knee bumping into his thigh. She looked incredibly vulnerable, even as naïve hope shone on her pretty face. "You can get help for this at the WTWA. They have support groups..."

He laughed harshly at even the suggestion of such a miracle. If miracles existed, Mutt would not be dead. Restless, he let go of her, stood. "Like you said, dwelling on the grief of what happened would only set me back. I want to move forward."

She rose with elegant grace. Her lower lip trembling, she pointed out, "Except you're not okay, Matt."

Wasn't that a little like the pot calling the kettle black? He lifted a censuring brow. "Projecting a little, are you?"

Sara flushed, indignant. "I'm trying to move on," she said, mimicking his coolly deliberate tone. "Build a new life for myself and Charley."

He tamped down his anger and resentment with effort. Shrugged. "Well, so am I."

His words hit their target.

Her face turned a blotchy pink. "I can't go back to living the way I did when Anthony was alive."

"I'm not asking you to."

She slammed her hands on her waist, and tilted her head up to his. "Aren't you?"

"First of all, I don't inflict my bad moods on you, which is why I'm trying to leave here tonight. Second, I'm not reckless."

"But," she interrupted, eyes glittering emotionally, "you are clearly suffering from post-traumatic stress."

He scoffed and leaned back against her front door, arms folded in front of him. "What makes you think that?"

She went utterly still for one long moment. "Besides the nightmares? The fact that you're not taking care of yourself as well as you should…a fact that was demonstrated when you let that splinter in your hand go untreated, even though it was clearly painful and you knew you were risking infection."

"I told you I would have gotten around to that. I delayed because I wanted to be with you."

Sara looked like the last thing she wanted was to be anyone's excuse.

Valiantly, she forged on, "You also avoid anything that reminds you of your loss. Like dogs."

"Hey," he said, smiling thinly, not about to criticized for that, "I managed to be around Champ."

She paced the foyer like a prosecuting district attorney before the jury. "But you weren't exactly comfortable at the WTWA reunion picnic, were you? All those servicemen and women. The dogs they loved…"

The memory caused his gut to twist.

He grimaced. "What's your point?" he demanded gruffly.

She stepped toward him, hands outstretched, like the relentless do-gooder she'd been when they'd met. "The point is I care about you, Matt, so much. Charley loves you. Champ adored you, despite the fact you avoided him as much as possible. And you cared about him. I saw it before we left for the picnic, when I realized—" her voice caught on a half sob, and it was a moment before she could go on "—we were going to have to say goodbye to him today." Eyes brimming with tears, she continued, "I know you, Matt. Not just on the surface, but deep down. You're meant to have a dog and a family of your own."

Matt only wished that were the case. He regarded her bleakly, his misery increasing by leaps and bounds. "Charley would probably tell you differently, given how I terrified him tonight."

She nodded then murmured softly, "Which is why I'm *suggesting* you get the help you need."

Except it wasn't really a choice. Not in her view, anyway. And the last thing Matt wanted was a repeat of his previous failed relationship. Or a new onslaught of the kind of badgering he'd received from his family. "Suggesting," he queried lightly in return. "Or commanding?"

Her shoulders stiffened in defiance. "I am not trying to order you around."

"Sure sounds like it," he scoffed.

Another tense silence fell. "I want to know you're taking care of yourself the way you should, Matt. I want you to be able to stay the night with me, to sleep here."

Matt wanted that, too. More than she knew. He also knew it wasn't going to happen. Because as hard as he tried, he couldn't just erase that part of his life. Couldn't will the nightmares away.

And he damn well wouldn't risk hurting or frightening her—or, God forbid, Charley—again.

Desperately trying to hang on to what they'd had, he countered just as persuasively, letting her know his own requirements for happiness. "And I want what we've had up to now, Sara. To live each day to the fullest and hang out together and help each other…and when we're both feeling it, make love with each other."

Her lips quivered as much as the rest of her. "I want that, too, Matt." Her eyes glistened with worry and hurt.

"I also want to know that you're not going to go off the rails, the way my husband did."

Was she talking about the accident that had cost Anthony his life? "I don't drive recklessly, or go into a curve traveling way too fast."

Sara swallowed, looking uncomfortable again. "I'm not talking about car wrecks, per se."

He studied her in confusion, sensing something new about to be revealed. "Then what are you talking about?"

Her breath caught. "Suicide."

Matt stared at Sara. "Anthony's death was ruled an accident. I know, because my brother Dan was the first deputy on the scene and I talked to him about it at the time."

Sara paused.

"You yourself told me tests showed there were no drugs or alcohol involved. He didn't have his cell phone with him, so he wasn't texting or looking at that. He was simply going too fast for the turn, and drove off the road. And that explanation makes sense. Given Anthony's postwar inclination toward reckless driving."

Looking terrified and distraught, and uncertain, she lamented, "But what if it was more than that?"

He shook his head at her. "Now you're the one going over the edge…"

She held up a hand, wordlessly asking him to hold on a minute. Then went to the computer set up on the desk in the living room. He'd never really seen her use it, he realized belatedly, as she turned it on and sat down in front of it. When the screen lit up, she motioned him over.

There were two different log-in icons on the desktop computer. She pointed to Anthony's, then typed in the password. His home screen came up. She clicked on the icon that held the Word documents and pulled up a list of files. They were arranged by date.

She clicked on one that was titled Pros and Cons.

When it came up, she sat back and motioned for him to read it over her shoulder. He moved in.

Under pros, it said:

1) Life insurance
2) Military benefits for surviving spouse
3) No more fights
4) No more regrets
5) No more worrying about not being the kind of dad our kid will need

Under cons, it said:

1) Will never know if it's a girl or a boy
2) Sara might never forgive me

Matt turned back to Sara in shock. This was damning, but not entirely conclusive. Unless she knew something else. "You think Anthony was struggling with whether or not to commit suicide?"

She got out of that document and opened up another file.

It appeared to be a personal letter, written six months before his accident.

Sara,
I'm so sorry. So very sorry...

Matt looked at her. "Did the two of you have a fight when he wrote that, an argument of some sort?"

She threaded her hands through her hair, pushing the

heavy length of it off her face. "I don't know what happened on that date. I've also gone back in my work calendar and so far as I can tell, that day was like any other."

"But something is nagging at you," Matt guessed, seeing her continued distress.

Sara nodded. "It was around that time that he told me he wasn't sure if we should keep trying to get pregnant. Maybe it wasn't a good idea for me to have a baby."

She shook her head, her sorrow clear. Tears of regret misted her eyes. Knotting her hands in front of her, she continued explaining softly, "That's all I'd been holding on to while he was overseas and I disagreed. He backed off and we kept trying but he became even moodier and more shut off, and… I don't know. As I mentioned before, our relationship wasn't good when he died. We'd become strangers, sharing the same house, sleeping in the same bed."

"Yes, I remember. I'm so sorry, Sara."

"So that letter he started and never finished, it could have been about whether or not we should have a baby…"

Or, Matt knew, it could have been the beginning of a suicide note that was also never written.

Sara reached for a tissue and blotted the dampness from beneath her eyes. "I don't think Anthony ever had nightmares. Not that I knew, anyway. But maybe it would have been better if he had, instead of stuffing all his conflict down, deep inside."

"So he came back from his tour in the Middle East with issues about what he saw and experienced there."

Sara gave a stiff, jerky nod.

"Did you ever tell anyone about this?"

"No. Just you."

"Why not?" he asked.

"Because he didn't want me to and I didn't have any proof of anything anyway, except he was closed off, moody, reckless. And none of that proved anything!"

She gestured impotently at the computer. "Don't you think if I thought there was even a chance he would do something crazy like take his own life that I would have found some way to intervene?"

Matt knew she would have.

"But I didn't think whatever was going on with him was anything that couldn't be fixed by opening up a new chapter in our lives."

"And starting a family," Matt guessed.

Wearily, she began to cry. "And I didn't come across these two files until about four and a half months after he died, and by then I was nearly six months pregnant. I didn't see any reason to speculate about what he had been thinking and feeling that day. I already felt guilty enough for sending him on the errand that led to the accident that caused his death." She shook her head in quiet misery. "I didn't want to burden anyone else with the question of what we will never know for sure."

Except, Matt thought, he was pretty sure Sara still had her suspicions. And those doubts were clearly tearing her apart. "I can see why you'd want to protect Charley," he said carefully.

She shoved her chair back, rose and gazed at him in a way that made his chest go tight. "Then you can also see why if you're going to be around us, as much as you have been, Matt, you have to get help dealing with your grief and guilt over Mutt's death."

A support group wasn't going to fix that.

Dwelling on it wasn't going to help.

He knew that. And somewhere, deep down, so did she.

Calmly and patiently he pointed out, "I can see why you're worried, but again, Sara, I'm *not* your late husband."

Her lips formed the stubborn line he knew so well. "I know that." She stepped toward him beseechingly. "But I also know that I can't take a chance that anything will ever happen to you." Tears streamed down her face. "I didn't do anything when it came to Anthony. I sensed he was in trouble. That he was shutting down. The same way your family and I have intuited you are privately struggling."

She shook her head, the mounting despair and fear emanating off her as she choked out, "I don't want to look back on this night and wonder what might have happened if only I'd been able to convince you to do what Anthony never would."

So this was it, then? he wondered furiously.

She told him how it was going to be and he was just supposed to forget what he wanted and needed—which was solitude and the time and space to heal on his own—and instead mindlessly cede to her demands?

"Look, Sara, I'm sorry for all you've been through. If I could undo it for you…and for Charley," he said, his voice catching, "I would."

She studied him, tears glistening in her eyes. Evidently sensing what he already knew—that they were at a crossroads. "But…?" she prodded shakily.

Knowing he had to be honest, even if it hurt, he looked her in the eye and went on implacably, "I won't be in a relationship where I'm told how, and where, to live my life. I did that and it didn't work. I was never more miserable." He shook his head, recalling, aware a line had been drawn, and she had drawn it. "I'm not doing it again," he said flatly.

Sara regarded him as if she could not believe he was countering her wishes. Even when she had given no notice to his. "So what are you saying, Matt?" she asked in shock, her eyes filling with tears.

The truth, Matt thought.

The sad, awful, heartbreaking truth.

That, as much as they both might have once wished it, the two of them were never meant to be.

And, given the fact they were oceans apart in what they each required to be happy, probably wouldn't be able to go back to friends with benefits, or mere friends, either.

Which left them with only one option.

He exhaled roughly and shook his head. "That it's over, Sara. You've made it clear. It has to be."

Bitterness and regret sweeping through him, he turned on his heel and left.

Chapter Fifteen

"Hey, stranger." Bess Monroe grinned as Sara walked into the WTWA facility. "Did you plan to attend tonight's support group for military widows?"

Was that tonight? she thought uncomfortably. Apparently so.

"Ah, no." Although Sara had been wondering...hoping, actually, that Matt might have decided to partake in the support group for returning veterans, which she definitely knew was being held this evening.

"I just came by to see if one of Charley's moccasin-style booties is here. He didn't have it on when we got home from the reunion picnic Saturday evening, and it wasn't in the car, so I thought someone might have found it here."

Bess gestured at one of the elevators. "Let's go to the Lost and Found and see."

Bess led her upstairs to the administrative offices. "So how've you been?" she asked, chatting amiably.

Horrible. "Good," Sara fibbed. She caught the rehab nurse assessing her with clinical expertise. "Why?"

Bess touched her arm gently. "You look tired."

Because I haven't been sleeping at all since Matt and I broke up. Not that we were actually a couple. Still, sometimes it felt as if we were.

Bess opened the storage room door. "I thought Charley might be getting another tooth."

Sara smiled wanly. "He is. But now that I've learned all the ways to ease his discomfort, he's okay most of the time."

"Good to hear." She pulled out a large plastic tub marked Lost & Found. "See it anywhere in here?"

Sara sorted through the collection of jackets and T-shirts, socks and shoes.

Bess perched on the edge of the desk with her arms folded in front of her. "So what is bothering you? I can tell it's something."

Finally, Sara thought, something they could talk freely about. She lifted her head. "I'm worried about Matt."

Bess was not surprised. "A lot of us are," she replied kindly. "Although he has seemed to be doing a lot better since he started hanging out with you and Charley."

Sara nodded. That was true, too.

Bess continued to study her. "Is Matt going to continue helping you and Charley out, now that Champ is with Alyssa Barnes?"

Sorrow pinched Sara's gut. "Probably not."

"Really?" The other woman blinked in surprise. "The two of them looked so cute together on Saturday. Almost like father and son!"

And what a good daddy Matt would be, Sara thought wistfully, if only things had worked out between the two of them. "I know." She bent her head and went back to looking through the bin.

Predictably, her friend, sensing trouble, did not give up her questioning. "So...what's going on?"

Should she say something or say nothing? Sara wondered. In the end, she couldn't risk doing nothing. Again. Even if doing nothing was meant to protect the ex-soldier in her life.

She swallowed around the ache in her throat and looked at Bess again. If anyone would know how to help, her friend the rehab nurse would. To her relief, Sara found that her affection for Matt gave her the courage she needed. "I found out Matt's been having nightmares related to his time in the Middle East."

"Does he talk about them?"

"Not really—" *not the way I'd like* "—and he doesn't want me to mention it, either." Which left a great big emotional wall between them. The kind so insurmountable it had torn them apart.

Bess nodded in understanding. "I'm guessing you suggested he talk to someone here."

"I did. And that did not go over well. He pretty much ended our, um—" *love affair* "—friendship," she said finally. Without warning, Sara spied what she had been searching for. She plucked the lost baby moccasin out of the box. "Here it is." Although she had gotten what she needed now, she continued sitting for a moment, suddenly too weary to move.

The last few days had taken a lot out of her.

In fact, she felt as depressed, deeply saddened and empty inside as she could ever remember feeling.

Bess moved next to Sara. She put an arm around her shoulders. "One of the things I've learned in my years as a rehabilitation nurse is that whenever trauma or tragedy occurs in a family, it hits *everyone* close to them, too." She paused to let her words sink in. "Even when the wounds aren't visible."

Sara blinked back tears and looked over at her friend. Bess took her hand, and they went to sit on the sofa along the wall.

Kindly, Bess explained. "Take Matt's brother, Jack, for instance. Jack's a civilian, but when his wife, Gayle, died during the birth of their third child, he was completely thrown by the loss, as were his kids."

Sara wiped her tears away. "But they've recovered."

Bess hesitated. "His situation is definitely a work in progress."

Which meant he had hope about reaching reconciliation. Whereas she…

"The point is, Sara, Jack knows he needs help after what happened. And he isn't afraid to ask for it."

Matt was in the pasture, tearing down old barbed wire fence with a vengeance, when he saw his mother's SUV driving across the field, toward him.

Knowing she'd likely heard through the Laramie grapevine that his "friendship" with Sara was kaput, he swore. Sensing a lecture of some sort was likely coming, he set his tools down, yanked off his leather gloves and strode toward her.

Rachel propped her hands on her hips. "And here I thought you were getting better."

He bypassed her and went straight for the big insulated water jug sitting on the bed of his pickup truck. "Thanks for the observation, Mom."

She watched him mop his face with his sleeve. "You're not returning messages again."

Matt tipped the jug and opened the spout, then drank deeply of the cold water. "Probably a reason for that."

"You don't want us to know you and Sara broke up."

Heart aching, he drank again. This time, to quell the sudden tightening of his throat. Feeling suddenly, unbearably, weary, he leaned against the side of his truck. "We were never a thing."

His mom scoffed, "Come on, now." Her expression as impatient as her voice. "Your family isn't that clueless. You were definitely a couple, even if you never identified it as such."

He didn't care what "evidence" his lawyer mother had uncovered. With a shrug, he turned his glance away. "It doesn't matter."

She narrowed her eyes at his terse words. "Why not?"

Matt sighed. Knowing the maternal inquisition would not end until he gave his mother something concrete to go on, he explained, "Because Sara found out I've had a few nightmares, and has demanded that I go to this support group at WTWA, and I'm not going to do it. I'm also not going to fight about it with her, so she and I are…not going to be friends or anything else anymore." It hurt, just saying the words.

Rachel nodded. "I see." A mixture of pity and disappointment gleamed in her eyes.

Matt knew Rachel didn't mean to judge him, but she was. Everyone was. He tensed all the more. "Look, Mom, I know you and Dad want me to be married and have a family," he began.

And part of me wants that, too. Or did. With Sara.

"And…?" Rachel prodded.

Matt spread his hands wide. Digging deep, he forced himself to be completely candid. "I want what you and Dad have. A relationship that's easy. That just works. And if I can't have that, then hell... I'm not going to have anything," he finished honestly.

His mother stared at him as if he'd grown two heads. "A relationship that's easy...that just works," she repeated in shock. She stepped nearer, her brows knit in confusion. "Is that what you think your father and I have?" she demanded.

Matt didn't know why she was so surprised. Sensing another critique coming on, he returned, "I know it is."

She matched his low, fierce tone. "Then you're wrong. Marriage only *looks* easy on the outside. When you're in it, it's anything but. A successful union takes work and effort and putting your partner's needs ahead of your own, and having them make the same sort of sacrifices for you. Because if you're both *giving* ninety-five percent, and *taking* five percent, a relationship will always work."

He understood selfless teamwork. It was what made military units thrive. "And that's what you and Dad do?"

"Yes," Rachel said softly. "We always put each other first. And we always will."

That made sense now that he thought about it. His parents were always helping each other out, caring for each other, loving each other, finding ways to make even the most contentious situation work out in a way that ultimately satisfied everyone. It was that kind of loving unity that had made their family thrive. Matt gulped. "I'm not sure Sara and I can do that, Mom. We're so different."

His mother offered a wry smile and shook her head. "Maybe not as much as you think. Given how stubbornly you're both behaving." She touched his shoulder with maternal affection. "Sara wants you to live life fully. She wants you to be able to sleep at night, to not be so shut off. Now tell me, Matt. What exactly is so wrong with that?"

"I know this was tough for you," the counselor said, as the group disbanded. She rose and intercepted Matt before he could get out the door. "But I'm happy you were here tonight, and happier still that you've also agreed to see one of our counselors, one-on-one."

"I appreciate the opportunity."

"It'll get better."

Will it? he wondered, thinking how he had initially let Sara down.

"Just give it time."

"I will," Matt promised. Because time was the one thing he suddenly had plenty of.

He ran into Bess Monroe as he headed down the stairs. She grinned at him, offering the encouragement, "Getting started is always the hard part!"

Bess was right. Taking advantage of all the WTWA had to offer hadn't been difficult, Matt thought. The really tough part was what was coming up next. Because he was on his way to the Blue Vista to see Sara.

Except…she wasn't at the ranch she'd shared with her late husband. She was here. In the flesh. Coming out of one of the *other* support group rooms. He blinked. "Sara?" he said hoarsely.

Surprise lit her pretty features. "Matt!" she said, coming to a halt right in front of him. Not looking nearly as unhappy to see him as he would have expected her to be, given the way they had parted several weeks ago. For a moment, her gaze devoured him, head to toe, as if checking for any further injury. She lightly clasped his arm. "I've been wanting to talk to you."

"Same here," he countered gruffly.

Bess passed them again and said, "My office is empty. Third floor."

Sara looked at Matt, an inscrutable question in her eyes. "Sounds good to me," he murmured. Whatever afforded them privacy.

They climbed the stairs, neither speaking until they got inside Bess's office and closed the door behind him.

Sara turned to face him, looking more gorgeous than ever in a pretty pink dress and white cardigan. "As you can probably see," she said, her intent gaze giving him courage, "I had my first group session."

"So did I," he forced himself to reveal with unflinching honesty.

Her breasts rose as she inhaled a shaky breath. "Wow."

"Yeah, wow." It had been a rough road, getting him to the recovery process, but now that he was here, he was not giving up. Not on healing. Not on her. Not on the two of them and the future he knew in his heart they were destined to have together.

"I guess great minds do think alike." Her eyes were kind. Hopeful...

He wrapped his arms around her waist and tugged her against him. "I'm sorry," he said hoarsely.

"I'm sorry, too. Really, really sorry. I was way too hard on you."

"You gave me the kick in the pants I needed."

She splayed her soft, delicate hands across his chest. Her palm settled over his rapidly beating heart. "The thing is, Matt, we both need help. I realize that now." Her lower lip trembled with emotion and her eyes sparkled with tears as she gazed up at him.

Shaking her head in silent regret, she confessed, "I

accused you of not wanting to deal with what happened when Mutt passed. Well, I haven't dealt with what happened when Anthony passed." Her low voice caught. "And I know that I have to do that before I have even a chance of moving on."

The heartache of loss was something they both shared. "I need to do that, too," he told her. The difference now was that grief was bringing them together, instead of driving them apart.

And together, he knew, they could do anything.

They continued staring at each other, breathing raggedly. Filled with hope.

"So...we're both getting counseling," Sara said, mulling that over with a mixture of satisfaction and relief.

"We are," he told her tenderly, taking her face in his hands and rubbing his thumbs over her cheeks. His throat felt tight and his easy speech deserted him. "But I don't want to just work on myself," he murmured softly. "I want to work on us, as a couple, too."

Sara blinked in amazement. "You do?"

"Yes, darlin'." He bent to kiss her, softly and sweetly, with all the tenderness she deserved. He paused, shook his head in remorse, admitting, "I've missed you more than words can say."

"Oh, Matt," Sara trembled in his arms. "I've missed you, too! So much!"

He gathered her close, and they kissed again, even more poignantly this time. With heartfelt regret, he admitted, "I never should have walked out the way I did, but," he paused to draw a breath, "our time apart reinforced something that deep down I think I've known all along."

"Which is...?" Sara asked, going completely still.

Matt sifted his hands through the silk of her hair, tilting her face up to his. "That you and I are made for each other. We might have our struggles and imperfections, but together we make sense."

Sara beamed with unmistakable happiness. "I couldn't agree more, Matt."

He nodded in relief. Knowing there was still more to work out, he forged on gruffly, "I want to do the things that will make our relationship selfless enough and strong enough to last a lifetime," he confessed raggedly, telling her all that he'd hidden, all that was in his heart. "Because I love you, Sara. With all my heart and soul."

"Oh, Matt," she whispered back joyously. "I love you, too!"

She lifted her head to his, and their lips met in a searing kiss that sealed the deal, and then another that was deeper and more long lasting, more passionate.

Finally, Matt drew back slightly. Grinning, he cleared his throat and drawled, "So now…for the *really* important part…"

She listened, ecstatic.

He took both her hands in his and clasped them tightly. "I want us to have a future together. You, me, Charley and whatever canine companions we bring into our lives."

Sara's smile brimmed, mirroring the happiness he felt. "Sounds perfect to me!"

He dropped down on one knee, ready and able to give her everything she ever wanted and needed. Solemnly, he asked, "Good enough to marry me when the time is right?"

"Oh, Matt," Sara whispered. She knelt and tugged him close. Their lips met in another sweet and enduring kiss. "There's nothing I want more!"

Epilogue

April, three years later...

"Mommy, when is my baby sister finally going to crawl?" Charley asked, his cute little face scrunched up impatiently.

"I don't know if Kristen will crawl," Sara told her son honestly as she set her six-month-old daughter on the play mat spread out over the living room floor.

Grinning, Matt picked up Charley and held him in his arms. The two handsome fellas went nose to nose. "You never did."

Charley blinked in amazement. "I didn't?"

Matt shook his head, then relayed proudly, "You went straight to walking."

"Wow," Charley breathed, and he and Matt settled on the floor next to Sara and the baby.

"Wow is right." Matt leaned over and bussed their

son's head. "Your mommy and I were really amazed when we saw you pull yourself up on the side of your crib and start walking along the rail."

Charley climbed onto Matt's lap and rested his hands on Matt's broad shoulders. Never at a loss for questions, asked, "How old was I, Daddy?"

Matt ran a hand lovingly over his back. "Eight months and two days."

Tilting his head, Charley considered. "Is that good?"

"Very good," Matt praised.

"I think Kristen will do very good, too," Charley pronounced solemnly. He got down to play with his baby sister. He showed her toys, and pretend-read to her from one of the cloth-covered infant storybooks.

Nearby, their adopted eight-year-old retired service dog, Mollie, watched happily from her cushion next to the fireplace, her big blond head nestled on her paws.

Looking every bit as contented as Sara felt, Matt settled closer to her, wrapped his arms around her waist, nuzzled her hair. "So what do you think, wife?" he murmured in her ear as their kids continued to play. "You want to grill out tonight, since the weather is so nice? Or go into town and eat?"

Aware it didn't matter what they did, because they were always incredibly happy when they were together as a family, Sara turned toward him and smiled. "Either option works for me, cowboy."

Soaking up his strong, masculine warmth, she wreathed her arms about his neck, kissed him on the cheek, then gazed adoringly into his gray-blue eyes.

It was amazing how much the support they had both received from the West Texas Warriors Association had not only helped them both resolve their own grief but helped others suffering from similar calamities heal as well.

She'd gone back to work part-time as a large-animal vet, and still shepherded a new litter of future service puppies into the world every year.

Matt had finished revitalizing his ranch and now ran a little cattle, alongside his brother's herd, too.

When they'd married, a year into their official courtship, she'd sold the Blue Vista and moved into his ranch house at the Silver Creek.

It hadn't taken long to convert the big empty space into their home, or for them to decide to expand their family. And now Charley and their dog, Mollie, and their new baby girl, Kristen, loved it there as much as she and Matt did.

To the point that life just didn't get any more perfect.

She smiled. "I think I'd like to stay here. Tomorrow is the service dog reunion. We still have a lot to do to get ready to host it, once the kids are in bed."

Matt grinned in easy agreement then winked. "And after that, I can think of another thing or two to do."

She laughed at the sexy mischief in his low tone. The soul-deep tenderness and affection in his smile. And felt an answering love filling her heart. "I can, too, cowboy," she whispered back playfully, kissing him again, slowly and sweetly. "I can, too…"

* * * * *

If you loved this story,
don't forget to check out the next book
in Cathy Gillen Thacker's beloved
Texas Legends: The Mccabes miniseries!

Lulu McCabe gets her very own love story
when she falls for fellow rancher Sam Kirkland
and they get the surprise of their lives!

Coming August 2019
from Harlequin Special Edition.

COMING NEXT MONTH FROM

◆ HARLEQUIN®

SPECIAL EDITION

Available April 16, 2019

#2689 A FORTUNATE ARRANGEMENT
The Fortunes of Texas: The Lost Fortunes
by Nancy Robards Thompson
After five years of working—and falling for—Austin Fortune, Felicity Schafer seems no closer to a promotion, or to getting Austin to open up. Will giving notice finally get Austin to *take* notice?

#2690 SWITCHED AT BIRTH
The Bravos of Valentine Bay • by Christine Rimmer
After finding out she was switched at birth, Madison Delaney heads to Valentine Bay to learn more about her birth family. She never expected to have feelings about Stren Larson, the shipbuilder who lives next door to her rental. But they come from such different worlds... Will they be able to see if those feelings can turn into forever?

#2691 HIS TEXAS RUNAWAY
Men of the West • by Stella Bagwell
Veterinarian Chandler Hollister has brought home many strays...but no one like lovely Roslyn DuBose. Exhausted, the single soon-to-be mom gratefully accepts his help. As one night becomes many days, Roslyn finds her way into Chandler's heart. But before this working man becomes a family man, Roslyn must face the one obstacle to their happy future: her secret past.

#2692 DOUBLE DUTY FOR THE COWBOY
Match Made in Haven • by Brenda Harlen
When Regan Channing finds herself pregnant, the last thing she expects is for another man to make her his wife! *Especially* not former bad boy Connor Neal. Pretty soon Regan's newborn twins have him wrapped around their fingers. But can the deputy's debt of obligation ever become true love?

#2693 THE CITY GIRL'S HOMECOMING
Furever Yours • by Kathy Douglass
Recent New York transplant Megan Jennings just found the ideal temporary home for sixteen suddenly displaced pets. Too bad the farm's owner isn't giving her the same warm welcome. A city girl broke Cade Battle's heart, and he refuses to trust the feelings Megan awakens. But Megan knows she's finally found her forever family. Can she make Cade believe it, too?

#2694 DEALMAKER, HEARTBREAKER
Wickham Falls Weddings • by Rochelle Alers
Big-city man Noah Wainwright has always viewed business as a game. But when he stumbles across bed-and-breakfast owner Viviana Remington, she's playing by different rules. Rules that bring the love-'em-and-leave-'em playboy to his knees... But when Viv learns how the Wainwright family plays the game, all bets are off.

HSECNM0419

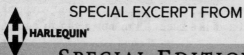
After the walk on the beach, she'd become overly polite
and distant. Knowing he wasn't going to sleep, Noah sat
up and tossed back the sheets. He found a pair of shorts
and slipped them on. Barefoot, he unlocked the screen
door and walked out into the night. He saw something
out of the corner of his eye and spied someone sitting on
the beach. A full moon lit up the night, and as he made
his way down to the water, he couldn't stop smiling.

She glanced up at him and smiled. "It looks as if I'm
not the only one who couldn't sleep."

Noah sank down next to her on the damp sand. Even in
the eerie light, he could discern that the sun had darkened
her skin to a deep mahogany. "I was never much of an
insomniac before meeting you."

Viviana pulled her legs up to her chest and wrapped her arms around her knees. "I'm not going to accept blame for that."

"Can you accept that I'm falling in love with you?"

Her head turned toward him slowly, and she looked as if she was going to jump up and run away. "Please don't say that, Noah."

"And why shouldn't I say it, Viviana?"

"Because you don't know what you're saying. You don't know me, and I certainly don't know you."

Don't miss
Dealmaker, Heartbreaker *by Rochelle Alers,*
available May 2019 wherever
Harlequin® Special Edition books and ebooks are sold.

www.Harlequin.com

Looking for more satisfying love stories
with community and family at their core?

Check out **Harlequin® Special Edition**
and **Love Inspired®** books!

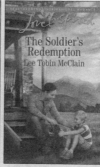

New books available every month!

CONNECT WITH US AT:

Facebook.com/groups/HarlequinConnection

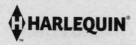

Facebook.com/HarlequinBooks

Twitter.com/HarlequinBooks

Instagram.com/HarlequinBooks

Pinterest.com/HarlequinBooks

ReaderService.com

◆ HARLEQUIN®

**ROMANCE WHEN
YOU NEED IT**

HFGENRE2018

Love Harlequin romance?

DISCOVER.

Be the first to find out about promotions,
news and exclusive content!

Facebook.com/HarlequinBooks

Twitter.com/HarlequinBooks

Instagram.com/HarlequinBooks

Pinterest.com/HarlequinBooks

ReaderService.com

EXPLORE.

Sign up for the Harlequin e-newsletter and
download a free book from any series at
TryHarlequin.com.

CONNECT.

Join our Harlequin community to share
your thoughts and connect with other
romance readers!
Facebook.com/groups/HarlequinConnection

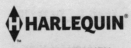

H HARLEQUIN®

**ROMANCE WHEN
YOU NEED IT**

HSOCIAL2018